Wrestling with Christmas

D to the Fourth Books & Scripts, LLC

Copyright ©2024 by Dewey Dellinger

Front Cover Design by: Syed Hassam

ISBN: 979-8-9907023-9-4

D to the Fourth Books & Scripts, LLC

Stanley, NC

United States of America

To Bill Burgin, a true and lasting friend, a great math teacher, a lover of *wraslin'*, and a wrestling opponent/partner (one of the Sharp Dressed Men, Paul Corona, Lord William Regal, Dirt/Rocky Rhodes). Although I'm not sure how he feels about romantic comedies, he would at least appreciate the wrestling component.

Wrestling with Christmas

Dewey Dellinger

TABLE OF CONTENTS

It Started with a Bell (Fifteen Years Ago)

Greg was fidgeting with his fingers, something he always did when he was nervous. The high school gym was noisy. Greg scoured the bleachers to see if his father was there. After a minute of scouring each row and section up and down, Greg's head drooped. He wasn't here … again. Greg's father had never attended one of his wrestling matches. Why should now be any different? His father had only attended one or two of Greg's football games but never a wrestling match. Greg took a deep breath to try to relax; he needed to clear his head and not let anything take his mind away from what he had to do.

Greg was in his senior year in high school. He had won the state championship in wrestling for his weight class the past two years, but winning it for the third year in a row would get him a scholarship to almost any university he wanted to attend. First, he had to get past the regional championships, and that's where he was today. This was the final match for the regional championship for his weight class.

Looking down the gym to the other team's bench, he could see his opponent for the match talking with the coach. The coach looked to know his business. He was gruff looking, which probably made him appear older than he really was. Greg guessed that the coach was in his late forties or early fifties.

His match would come up soon, and he fidgeted some more and did some final stretches. Multiple matches were occurring simultaneously on the many mats stretched out on the gym floor. The match on the mat he would wrestle on was in its last period.

Greg's coach slapped him on his shoulders. "You can do this."

Coach Harris Bell had coached wrestling for over twenty years at the high-school level. He looked down toward the opposing team's bench and saw a tall and lanky but muscular Greg Hunter. Coach Bell knew his wrestler would have his work cut out for him. Greg was the best wrestler in the state in his weight class. Coach Bell turned to Steve Ross. "Now listen,

Steve. This guy is one of the top wrestlers in the state. He's won the state championship the past two years. Remember what we talked about from studying the video footage and from his previous matches."

"I remember coach, I got this."

Coach Bell thought Steve's reply was just a tad bit too cocky. But then everything about Steve was cocky, arrogant, and self-centered. This was not the guy Coach Bell wanted dating his sixteen-year-old daughter, Jennifer. They say opposites attract, but why this guy? Although Jennifer was only sixteen, she had a certain maturity about her that made her seem older. She was bookish, which was good … to an extent. But she had a heart of gold, was down-to-earth, and was very family oriented. She was a little too much on the shy side, but hopefully, she would grow out of that. Jennifer was at the match, but she didn't like wrestling. He wasn't sure whether she was there to support him or Steve, probably both. The coach cast a glance at his daughter. There she was, writing in her journal … again. That's all she seemed to do lately.

Greg began making his way down the side. He would have to pass by the other team's bench, and no doubt several taunts from them, to get to the mat on the far end of the gym. As he was walking, a pretty, teenage girl with shiny brownish auburn hair caught his eye. He found himself mesmerized by her. She didn't see him though because she was writing in a notebook. Realizing he had lost his concentration, he began once again to get his mind into his match. He was now focused so much on his match that he didn't see her move into his path. The resulting collision jarred his concentration. The girl was startled, and the collision had caused her to drop her notebook. Greg stooped down, picked it up, brushed it off, and handed it to her. Her hazel eyes momentarily took his breath away. "I'm sorry," he heard himself say. "I didn't mean to bump into you. Here you go," he added as he handed her the notebook. She simply stared back at him without saying a word.

Jennifer was caught off guard when the wrestler from the opposing team bumped into her. She was so busy writing that she had not noticed that she had moved directly into his path.

She was embarrassed and didn't know what to say when he handed her journal to her. As he dashed away, she kicked herself mentally for not saying something, anything. Jennifer looked up and noticed her father looking at her with a smile on his face. Steve and the wrestler who bumped into her were headed for the mat. "He's really cute. What's his name?" she asked her dad.

"That's Greg Hunter."

Jennifer didn't know why he was so appealing to her; she had a boyfriend, and she felt guilty for the betrayal.

The match was underway, but Coach Bell couldn't help but think about what he had seen. Both Greg and Jennifer seemed really attracted to each other. Although Greg and his daughter were from different suburbs in the Cincinnati area, he wished they were in the same school rather than his daughter and Steve. Coach Bell prided himself on his instincts, and his instincts were telling him that Greg was a good guy. As the match began, he even found himself secretly pulling for Greg over his own wrestler, Steve. Greg was a tremendous wrestler, one of those once-in-a-decade wrestlers who had an innate, natural ability. He had seen Greg wrestle against his team before and wished he could have been his coach. In all honesty, Greg was one of the best wrestlers he had ever seen. His thoughts were interrupted when he saw the referee tap the mat with his hand, indicating a fall. After only one minute into the first period of the match, Greg had pinned Steve's shoulders to the mat for a two-count to win the match.

Coach Bell could tell that Steve was angry. He quickly stormed off the mat and breezed right by him.

"Come on, Jennifer. Let's go," growled Steve.

"But I want to stay to support my father," she replied.

Coach Bell didn't know if that was true or if she just wanted a chance to see Greg again.

"I said, let's go!" Steve grabbed Jennifer's arm pulling her away.

Coach Bell burned with anger at Steve's behavior, and alarm bells went off in his mind warning him that no good would come from their relationship. He started to go after them, but he knew that would only irritate Jennifer. While the hairs on his arm were still bristling, Greg walked by. "Great match, Mr. Hunter. You're one of the best wrestlers I've ever seen. Good luck at the state championships."

"Thanks, Coach." Greg hesitated and looked around.

She's not here, unfortunately, thought Coach Bell. Apparently not seeing who he was looking for, Greg made his way to his teammates and huge display of congratulatory remarks and celebration.

Son of Hunter Savage (Present Day)

Jennifer Bell stood at the front of her fourth-grade classroom in an elementary school in one of Cincinnati's suburbs. She had just finished the lesson for the day with about one minute before the bell would ring signaling the end of the period. As a teacher in her seventh year, she knew that every ounce of class time must be used, else students' attention would wander. "Rehearsals for this year's Christmas play begin next week. If anyone wants to participate, I have consent forms that you can take home to have signed by a parent or guardian."

The bell rang, and several students grabbed forms on their way out of the classroom. Almost immediately, two boys, Tommy McElroy and Bobby Schrum began taunting Austin Hunter. This was not the first time the two had picked on Austin, but the taunts were becoming more frequent as Austin had become more withdrawn.

"Your dad is not Hunter Savage," teased Tommy menacingly.

"He is too!" lashed out Austin.

"Then why isn't your last name *Savage?*" taunted Bobby.

"Yeah, and you're too puny to be the son of Hunter Savage," chimed Tommy.

Jennifer quickly ran in between the boys. "I've had enough of this goading," warned Jennifer. "You boys know that you are expected to leave the room quickly and quietly."

"Austin claims that his father is the World Wrestling Champion, Hunter Savage," explained Tommy.

As if that were enough to excuse their behavior, thought Jennifer.

"He is my father," rebutted Austin.

"Go to your next class with no further talking," warned Jennifer.

"Yes ma'am," replied all three boys.

Starting from almost the beginning of the school year, Austin had been saying that his father was the world wrestling champion. His belief had seemed harmless at first; almost all of the kids still had vivid imaginations, and she certainly did not want to stifle them. But she also didn't want to see kids suffer emotionally either.

The three boys exited the classroom, and, almost as if on cue, Hellen Collins, a fourth-grade math and science teacher entered Jennifer's classroom. Helen was a year or two older than Jennifer. One of her special skills was putting Jennifer's teeth on edge with the regularity of laxative medication. Just because she and Helen were competitive with each other was no reason for her to think badly of Helen, and she didn't think that Helen was a bad teacher. In fact, Helen was last year's Teacher of the Year. Jennifer knew she shouldn't be jealous of her colleague, but she was. Helen was often flirtatious, and Jennifer had seen her flirt with the school principal and the system superintendent, who were on the committee that selected last year's Teacher of the Year.

"What was that ruckus about?" inquired Helen with a sugary innocence.

Here it comes, thought Jennifer.

"You know that as the district teacher-of-the-year, I could give you some pointers on classroom management."

Jennifer could feel the blood rushing to her head and her face reddening at Helen's comment. She felt chastised. Jennifer ground her teeth. "I've been teaching almost as long as you have, Helen, and I generally do pretty well managing my classroom."

"Just making an offer." Helen's gaze diverted to what Jennifer was holding in her arms. "What's that you're holding?"

"It's this year's Christmas play. I was trying to drum up interest since rehearsals start soon." Jennifer clung tightly to the security blanket of the manuscript in her arms.

"What Christmas play are you doing this year?"

As if Helen really cared. "Oh, it's new, something I wrote myself."

An almost unnoticeable smirk formed on Helen's lips. "That's cute. You know. There are plenty of plays we've used over the years that you could have picked that were **professionally** written. You didn't have to try to come up with something on your own."

That patronizing … Jennifer wouldn't complete the thought. Santa Claus is watching, she quickly thought to herself. She laughed at herself for thinking this, but it was close to Christmas, and it was her way of reminding herself to be good. Her mother used that on Jennifer when she was a young girl, and it just carried over. Just because she and Helen were competitive with each other and were both in their early thirties was no reason for her to think badly of Helen. That was twice now in the span of a minute that she had reminded herself not to think badly of Helen!

"We need to get you on some dates so that you're not cooped up all the time at home. I went on a date with the mayor this weekend. Maybe I could set you up with one of my previous dates. I dated our local state legislator. He wasn't my type, but you might like him."

Jennifer tried not to be derailed by the dating discussions that Helen often used as a passive taunt against her. Helen always seemed to go out with well-to-do men. Jennifer rarely dated since her breakup, even though she felt she was as attractive as Helen. There's still plenty of time for that, she thought to herself; I'm only thirty-one. She told herself one more time that Santa Claus was watching so that she would guide her thoughts in more productive ways. "Thank you,

Helen. I don' t really like set up dates. I'll find someone when the time is right."

"Just making an offer."

That night, Jennifer thought she would pay Austin's mother, Stephanie Hunter, a brief visit. They lived only a few houses away, in the same nice neighborhood in a nice suburb about twenty minutes from Cincinnati. Jennifer visited with Stephanie on numerous occasions, but she still didn't know a lot about her. Stephanie had moved into the neighborhood right at the time the school year was ready to start. She knew Stephanie was a divorced mom and a Vice President at a marketing firm in Cincinnati.

Jennifer put on a coat and walked the short distance to Stephanie's house. She rang the doorbell and Stephanie answered.

"Hi, Jennifer. Come in. It's cold outside. Did you walk here?"

"It is cold, but I'm not going to drive when I live just a few houses down," Jennifer remarked as she went inside.

"Of course you wouldn't drive. I'm still not used to the temperature here, after spending so many years in Florida. Are you just visiting, or is this school-related?"

"School-related, unfortunately. Austin's still having a difficult time with some of the other kids." Jennifer noticed the harried expression on Stephanie's face. Each time she had one of these conversations with a single parent, a pang of empathy tugged at her heart. Although she didn't have children of her own, she knew that parenting was difficult. Being a single parent while working full-time was an entirely different level of parenting. Jennifer couldn't imagine how single working parents managed.

"Would you care to have a seat?" asked Stephanie.

"Thank you, but I only plan to stay a minute or two. "

"I know it's only been a few months since we moved here from Florida, but I hoped Austin would be doing better by now. He misses my parents and his friends. He's had such a tough time trying to make new friends here."

Jennifer was unsure about how to approach the next part. Telling parents about a child's imagination was often a tricky business. "He seems to be in a make-believe world, thinking his dad is the world wrestling champion. The other boys make fun of him for it."

A slight enigmatic smile briefly formed on Stephanie's face before she quelched it. "It's true. Austin's father is the world wrestling champion."

Jennifer was shocked at the revelation and hoped her face hadn't betrayed her too much. "I've never heard you mention your ex-husband. You mean Austin's dad really is Hunter Savage?"

"I probably haven't talked about him because he is rarely around. Hunter Savage is his stage name. His real name is Greg Hunter, but that doesn't sound as good of a ring name as Hunter Savage. Do you actually watch wrestling?"

Jennifer was taken aback by the question. It was almost as if she were asked if she participated in some scandalous or socially unacceptable activity. "Oh, no. I have heard Austin talk about him so much. That's how I know the name. My dad coaches wrestling at the high school, but I don't watch the tv stuff."

"Austin hasn't seen his father since we've moved here, but Greg is still Austin's hero. To Austin, he can do no wrong. Greg and I have been divorced for seven years, and I've raised Austin pretty much myself, even when we were still married."

Jennifer was unsure of what to say to Stephanie's revelation. "I'm sorry. I didn't know, but that doesn't change the fact that Austin is struggling socially. Things seem to be getting worse. In P.E., the kids don't want him on their teams. I just wanted to bring this to your attention. I don't want to see him draw into himself. Maybe you can talk with Austin."

"Thanks, Jennifer. I will. It's been really nice having you so close by."

Jennifer turned to leave. She reached the door when an idea suddenly sprang into her mind. "I just had a thought. I'm directing the school Christmas play this year. Maybe you can convince Austin to take part in it. I know it's a small thing, but it might help give him some interactions with other kids."

"I'll nudge him in that direction. Thanks again, Jennifer."

Later than night, Stephanie talked with Austin about what he had been going through. Austin had not mentioned the taunts of the boys at school, and she thought he was just having a difficult time adjusting after the move. Austin cried, which caused her to cry, when he talked about how out of place he had been feeling and how he was not getting along with the others in his class, especially the boys. None of them believed that Hunter Savage was his father, and he felt as though they had been picking on him relentlessly. He had asked her when his dad was going to see him again, and if his dad liked him. Inside, Stephanie was fuming at Greg, but she was trying to defend him to Austin and convince Austin that his father did indeed care for him.

She felt guilty afterwards for not having learned this from Austin sooner. She poured herself a glass of wine to soothe her nerves. Working as a Vice President in a new job while being a single parent was difficult, to say nothing of adjusting and re-establishing herself after the move. There were still boxes in the upstairs guest bedroom that had yet to be unpacked.

The Best Player in the Game

Greg Hunter, or Hunter Savage as he was known to wrestling fans, was at the pinnacle of his career as World Heavyweight Champion of the Global Wrestling Organization, or GWO as it was sometimes called. He was one of the best in the business, having been world champion on multiple occasions and currently holding the record as the longest reigning world champion in GWO history.

He sat alone backstage in his dressing room as he waited for his interview and his match. He wore his regular tight-fitting T-shirt. On the front of the shirt were pictures of five playing cards showing the world championship belt on each card. Above the cards was his catchphrase, *The Best Player in the Game*.

Yet, rather than concentrating on the upcoming match, his thoughts drifted to his son as they generally did before a big live-streaming event. He looked at a picture of Austin on his phone. A heavy cloud of guilt came upon him. Before big events were some of the few times he thought about his family. Why did that aways tend to happen? From the recesses of his mind came the memories of the times when he was in high school and always looked for his father before big matches. His father wasn't there either just like he was not there for Austin. He wasn't cold-hearted; he was always traveling. *Always* being the key word. He was on the road over three hundred days a year, but the memories and loneliness always caught up with him at major wrestling events. His thoughts swirled in a whirlwind of remorse and *what ifs*.

Greg tried to shake his head clear of the thoughts that were haunting him. I'll think of something else, he thought to himself. I hope I land the movie role I auditioned for. Then, I won't have to rely so much on wrestling. He hoped to follow in the footsteps of other wrestlers turned actors like The Rock, Dwayne Johnson. Of course, there were others, John Cena and Dave Batista, to name a few. At thirty-three years of age, he definitely wasn't old, but if he was going to make the move to acting, he needed to do it sooner rather than later. He really wasn't conceited, but he knew he was handsome and muscular, two great qualities for the action adventure-type roles he wanted.

Almost as if his thoughts manifested it, Greg's phone rang. The caller id showed that his agent was calling. He had the stereotypical agent, fast-talking, persuasive, and the kind of used cars salesman persona that made you think you were the most important person in the world at the moment. Greg pressed the icon to answer, and his agent immediately began talking before Greg could even acknowledge that he had answered the call.

"Greg, buddy. The lead role of Alan Quartermain in the remake of *King Solomon's Mines* is between you and one other person. They liked your audition. We should know something in a few weeks. Look good in your match tonight."

His agent had disconnected before Greg was able to say a word, and that was saying something!

Greg returned to looking at Austin's picture on his phone. Thoughts of his son came racing to him. How long had it been since he had seen Austin, over six months ago? No wonder his ex-wife Stephanie was constantly on him to see Austin; he couldn't blame her. He used to say that he was wrestling for the money to help Stephanie and Austin, but Stephanie called his bluff quickly and effectively. He couldn't blame her for that either. Face it, Greg. Family always lets you down. The only person you can count on is yourself. That's why he had to remain popular. That's why he needed this movie deal. He didn't want to face, wouldn't even think, about what would happen if his popularity suddenly disappeared. Although the job was grueling, he had always enjoyed wrestling. When he was a kid, he always liked wrestlers with larger-than-life personas, wrestlers such as John Cena, Seth Rollins, Roman Reigns, Randy Orton, R-Truth, Kofi Kingston, Sheamus, Cody Rhodes, Daniel Bryan, A.J. Styles, The Miz, and older generation wrestlers such as The Rock, Triple H, Stone Cold Steve Austin, Chris Jericho, and Booker T. Each generation had its own stars, just as he was now for some generation … for his son.

Three women in their twenties came to Greg's dressing room.

"Hey, Greg. I mean Hunter. We go on in five minutes for the promo interview. Did you not hear the Live Events Director? You look like you are a thousand miles away."

"Oh, hi Misty. I was just thinking about my son. I always think about him before big events."

"Aw … that's sweet," gushed Misty. "How old is he?"

"Nine. I think. With all the traveling I do with wrestling, I don't get to see him much."

"We'd better go to the interview area," urged Sherry.

The three women, Misty, Sherry, and Anna, served as eye candy for Greg's wrestling alter ego. Hunter Savage was a playboy who enjoyed the finer things of life, fine clothes, fine cars, and fine women. He was almost always interviewed surrounded by two or three women. They weren't girlfriends of his, just women to help create the illusion of him as a playboy. Misty, Sherry, and Anna had been with him for the past few months, but others had served in that role previously. Misty was actually the niece of Tony, the interviewer and commentator for the organization. Sherry was the daughter of the owner, and Anna was the wife of one of the wrestlers. The three women were like co-workers. The real Greg Hunter, not the wrestling persona, was not like his alter ego. He liked fine cars, but that was about as close as he got to his persona. He hadn't dated in … well, not since the last time he had seen his son, and that relationship didn't last but a couple of months. He always seemed to use the last time he had seen his son as a time reference for everything.

"I think I'm ready." Greg threw the ten-pound world wrestling championship belt across his shoulder. He always debated whether to drape the belt across his shoulder or wear it. Maybe I'll wear it around my waist this time, he thought. He transferred the belt from his shoulder to around his waist. Turning the buckle in front, he fastened it, and then spun it around his waist so that the large emblem on the belt was clearly displayed.

"Where are your sunglasses?"

Greg patted his body, including the top of his head, searching for his expensive sunglasses. He almost always wore them, even inside. "How do I always lose my sunglasses just before I have to go on camera?"

"Did you leave them in your dressing room again?" chided Sherry.

Greg hurried to his dressing room and scoured the room. There they were, lying on a table. He quickly grabbed them and rejoined the three ladies who would accompany him. "You know I need these to keep from being blinded by the flashy dresses you three have."

"Just be that witty on camera!" retorted Misty.

"I always am." Greg was proud at being able to readily come up with a quip. He joined arms with Misty and Sherry.

Anna traipsed along beside the three. Greg was mentally getting into character as they proceeded out of the room to go to the interview. As was customary before a major match, the wrestlers would hype up the crowd for the upcoming events. "What city are we in?"

"Philadelphia!" the three women chided in unison.

Off the Top Rope

Almost six hundred miles away from the wrestling event in a suburb about twenty miles outside of Cincinnati, nine-year old Austin was in the kitchen carefully sneaking two cookies out of a glass covered plate. He opened the refrigerator, took out a carton of milk, and poured himself a glass of milk. Returning the milk carton to the refrigerator and carefully closing the door, he made his way into the living room where he had the television turned to wrestling. He sat cross-legged on the floor and took a big bite out of a chocolate chip cookie. "Mom! Come quick. Dad's about to talk," cookie crumbs spewing from his mouth as he yelled.

Thirty-three-year-old Stephanie Hunter lumbered into the room carrying a basket full of laundry. Tiredness from her day job coupled with her nightly routine of raising a son on her own, showed on her attractive face. "You don't have to call me every time he's on tv. He says the same thing every time." She spied the cookie crumbs on the floor before she saw the plate of cookies in Austin's lap. "How many cookies have you had?

"Just these two, mom."

Stephanie's attention turned to the television, where her ex-husband, Greg Hunter, aka Hunter Savage, stood with three flashy-dressed women. The handsome world champion wore one of his trademark T-shirts and expensive sunglasses. Hunter Savage ran his fingers through his blond hair on both sides of his head and turned to Tony the commentator. Stephanie had met Tony on one occasion. He was rather unimpressive at the time, but in his suit and booming broadcaster voice, he had transformed into character just as easily as Greg had transformed into Hunter Savage. Tony held the microphone up to a taller Hunter Savage, who snatched it away in demonstrative fashion.

"Tony, I've said it before. I'm the best player in the game, and the hand I've been dealt is the World Championship Belt!" The three women leaned in closer to Hunter Savage as he spoke.

"There you have it wrestling fans," boomed Tony. "Hunter Savage, the longest reigning world champion in the history of the Global Wrestling Organization franchise. He'll be in the main event here at *Smacksgiving* where he faces his long-time nemesis, Rocky Rhodes. It's all coming up in a few minutes!"

Stephanie stifled a laugh. She didn't know what was the funniest, Hunter's theatrics, the women's flashy costumes and ogling, or the fanciful name of *Smacksgiving* for this wrestling event. Of course, she had heard the name, *Smacksgiving*, for years. It was generally held around Thanksgiving. She wondered if someone's job was to actually come up with names for wrestling events. Her attention turned from amusement back to Austin, who was eagerly awaiting the match. "Honey, have you done your homework yet?"

"Aw, mom! The match is going to start in a few minutes. You know this is the only time I get to see Dad."

Stephanie hesitated. She was torn in her role as a mother. She knew that what Austin said was true for the most part, but the other part of her was concerned about her son doing well in school. He seemed to be having a tough time this year in the fourth grade. She knew the move from Florida had been especially tough on him. Not seeing his father since they arrived, especially since they were near where Greg grew up, had been especially tough. Finally, one part of her won over the other. "All right, but it's off to bed as soon as the match is over, and tomorrow, we're going to sit here until your homework is done." She hoped she had made the right choice.

Trancelike, her son merely nodded with the remainder of the cookies stuffed into his mouth while he guzzled milk, leaving a faint milk mustache over his upper lip.

Stephanie walked over and sat in a chair. Her attention turned to the basket of laundry that needed folding before she could go to bed. Vaguely, she heard the bell ring, indicating the start of the match. She didn't know how much time had elapsed when she heard Austin groan. At first, she wondered if he had eaten too many cookies and had an upset stomach. She studied at Austin, but his attention was fully on the television. Her eyes migrated to the tv screen where she watched a replay of Hunter Savage jumping off the top rope. As he landed, his knee buckled under him, and he fell to the mat. He was holding his knee and was in obvious pain. As live action resumed, the referee stopped the match, and she watched as medics came into the ring.

"Dad's hurt! The referee stopped the match."

Stephanie looked up from the laundry she was folding. "I'm sure he will be okay. We've talked about this before. Wrestling is a lot of show. I'm sure he will be alright." She said this to try to alleviate Austin's concern for his father, but she could tell that this wasn't part of the show. Hunter Savage, or

Greg, was in pain, and the referee would not have stopped the match if it weren't serious.

Training Time

The next day, Stephanie was at her job in downtown Cincinnati where she was the Vice President at a prestigious marketing firm. She was already tired from getting to bed late due to the wrestling match. She wondered how much more tired she would have been if the match had lasted as long as it should have. She had to get up early every school day to take Austin to school before the twenty-minute, or more, drive to work. At the moment, all she could think about was the large caramel latte with a double shot of espresso that sat on her desk. She could almost hear the caffeine singing a siren's song to lure her near. As she was about to take a sip its promising alertness, the Branch President of the marketing firm, Ms. Sterne, stuck her head in Stephanie's office.

The sweet siren song immediately popped out of her head when she heard her boss's voice. Stephanie looked up and saw her boss' head sticking into her office like a cuckoo in a cuckoo clock. Her boss, Ms. Sterne, was appropriately named. Stephanie didn't think she had ever seen Ms. Sterne smile, let alone laugh. Ms. Sterne was in her late fifties with a no-nonsense persona.

"Are you getting ready for your three-week training at corporate headquarters in London? You'll be leaving soon."

"Yes. I'm ready."

"Is that the Atchison report you're holding?"

Stephanie consciously felt her eyes looking down to make sure. "Yes, Ms. Sterne."

"May I see the report?" Ms. Sterne came into the office and sat in a chair near Stephanie's desk.

"Of course," Stephanie answered, handing her the report.

Ms. Sterne flipped through the report quickly, but Stephanie knew that even with a quick perusal, Ms. Sterne would be as familiar with the report as she was.

"Impressive work, as usual."

"We'll miss you in the short time you'll be away, and I'll try to keep the work from piling up so that you won't have too much to catch up on when you return. I'll work with your assistant, Allie, to make sure of it. I know you don't really need this training, but it's company policy. I don't have a family myself, but I realize that this in an inconvenience for you."

"I knew about the training when I accepted this job, and I've made plans for my parents to watch my son while I'm gone."

"I would not have thought otherwise."

An Ounce of Prevention

Jennifer Bell looked out the window of her fourth-grade classroom at the students who were outside during their lunch period. Some were playing basketball. Others were running around in a game of tag. Others were just in various cliques, talking. A few were reading. The school allowed fourth and fifth grade students an extended lunch period of fifteen minutes to give the children some additional time for physical and social activity, almost like a recess time. Although most schools only offered physical education classes as a means for physical activity, Jennifer was glad the school offered the additional time separate from physical education because it helped increase the children's attention after lunch, in her opinion.

The fourth and fifth grade teachers took turns monitoring recess, but today wasn't her turn. Still, she kept an eye on the students through her window when it was Helen Collins turn at recess duty. Helen was very extroverted and very talkative. Her attention would sometimes be focused on a conversation with a fellow teacher rather than on the group of students during recess.

A noise outside interrupted her thoughts, and she drifted over to a different window to get a better view and to see what the commotion was. Several of the boys in her class were gathered around Austin Hunter, and she immediately rushed off to go outside before the situation escalated. As Jennifer approached the group of boys gathered around Austin, she could hear them taunting him.

"Still say your dad is Hunter Savage after what happened last night?" mocked Tommy McElroy. Tommy's chest puffed out, and he positioned his body into Austin's personal space.

Bobby Schrum added to the taunting. "He couldn't even finish his match because he got hurt. I guess you're a loser like him." Bobby was taller than Austin and was looking down his nose at him.

"He didn't lose. The referee stopped the match. My dad is still the world champion."

The boys began to chide in union, "Loser. Loser."

Austin appeared to be at a breaking point, and he balled up his fists.

"What are you going to do?" questioned another boy that Jennifer didn't know, "fight us?"

"Boys, that's enough!" scolded Ms. Bell. "Go over and stand with Ms. Collins, and I don't want to hear another word of this conversation." She didn't think they would actually get into a fight, but an *ounce of prevention* as the saying went.

"Boys will be boys," remarked Helen as Jennifer walked over to her.

"Will you watch them until recess is over?" Jennifer didn't know if she could trust Helen Collins even with that simple task, but she had little choice.

"Okay," affirmed Helen. "Somone's in trouble," she said turning to the group of boys.

"And none of you say a word for the remainder of recess," warned Jennifer. The verbal exchanges with Austin and the other kids were indeed escalating.

Reluctantly, Jennifer made her way over to Stephanie's house that night. Although she hated going again so soon, she felt she needed to apprise Stephanie of the day's events at school. Jennifer rang the doorbell and was once again invited inside by Stephanie. This time she sat in order to appear more polite.

"I hate he's being picked on like that," lamented Stephanie upon hearing the story. "This couldn't come at a worse time."

"Why is that?" asked Jennifer curiously. Was there ever a good time for this type of thing?

"As part of taking the Vice President job, I agreed to take a three-week training in London by the end of the calendar year."

"You can't take Austin out of school that long!" exclaimed Jennifer.

"Oh, I'm not. My parents are coming up to stay with him. I wish I could do the training another time, but as I said earlier, it must be completed by the end of the year. I needed to be with Austin for a few months when we moved, and I definitely want to be home at Christmas. That didn't leave too many choices."

"I think you're right about that. I don't think Austin would have handled it very well at all, if you had gone on the training sooner. I'll do my best to keep an extra eye on him while you're away."

"Thank you, Jennifer. You know … after the new year, I'll invite you over some. We ought to have some social visits rather than school-related ones."

"That would be nice. I'd like that."

Mancave

Greg had a small apartment in New York City where the Global Wrestling Organization was headquartered. His apartment wasn't in one of the more expensive areas of the city. It didn't need to be; Greg was rarely there. Greg was more practical when it came to living arrangements so that he could splurge in other areas, if he wanted to. The fact was, Greg rarely splurged in other areas either. He didn't have a car; he didn't need one in New York. When he traveled to wrestle, he mostly flew, or rode in one of the GWO buses if the wrestling venue wasn't too far away. About the only thing he spent money on was the child support he sent to Stephanie. His father had been very frugal, and Greg supposed he picked that up naturally from him. Although the apartment was small, Greg liked it, and he had turned it into his mancave. Framed wrestling magazine covers with him on the cover adorned the walls. Several wrestling belts were displayed in showcases. Greg didn't have all the wrestling belts he had won; the GWO kept them for the next champion. But every so many years, the belts would be replaced or the title would change names. For example, the North American Heavyweight Championship belt was renamed the United States Heavyweight Championship belt, or if the World Championship belt was over so many years old and needed updating. When those kinds of things happened, the GWO would allow the wrestler holding the belt to buy the belt, which Greg did. His high school and collegiate wrestling trophies along with his Olympic medal were openly displayed on various bookcases.

Greg was icing his knee before he had to go in later that afternoon for his appointment with the GWO doctor when his phone rang. He reached for it on a nearby table, grimacing as the movement put pressure on his knee. The caller id showed *Stephanie*. Stephanie and he would call each other occasionally, but it was by no means an ordinary occurrence. Greg touched the screen to answer the call. "Hi, Steph. What's up?"

"I'm at work, but I wanted to call to see if you're ok or if your injury was part of the script. Austin is concerned."

"Unfortunately, it wasn't part of the script. I was hurt. I see the doctor today, but it's feeling a little better. I'm icing it as we speak. Hopefully, it's nothing that a little physical therapy won't cure. Did I tell you that I auditioned for the remake of *King Solomon's Mines*? It's an action-adventure movie. My audition went great, and I think I have a good shot at getting the part."

"Congratulations," came the response at the other end. "Look, there's another reason I'm calling. I have to leave for my training next week. My parents are going to come up and watch Austin. I was thinking that if you were out due to your injury that you might want to watch him instead of them. You haven't seen him since we moved, and to be honest, he's having a difficult time adjusting here. I think you could help him; I haven't seemed to be able to, and I've never seen him like this before."

"If your parents can watch him, that would be great. I imagine they are ready to visit and are probably looking forward to spending some time with him. My contract ends at the end of the year. I need to get ready for the next pay-per-view streaming event, *Winter Frenzy*. If I don't get the movie role, I really need to have a good showing, or it might affect my wrestling contract. Plus, the doctor may clear me to wrestle next week."

"I knew it was a longshot," sighed Stephanie, "but if you change your mind today or tomorrow, let me know. Listen, I know popularity is important to you, and I know this is not your favorite time of the year. Whether you watch Austin or not, you need to see your son soon."

"I will. Bye, Steph."

Had he really not seen Austin since they moved from Florida to Cincinnati? Greg couldn't believe how time flew by. But that had to be right. He had seen Austin in June, and Stephanie and Austin moved at the first of August. He needed to see Austin soon but when? Maybe between *Winter Frenzy* and the start of filming, if he got the role ... unless filming started early. If he did get the role and if filming started early, there would be no telling when he could go see Austin. Even if he did get a chance to see Austin before *Winter Frenzy*, what could he do that would help Austin in a couple of or a few days? Well, he would think about that later. He needed to get ready to head to GWO Headquarters to see the doctor.

A Great Ride and a Big Favor

The day after the wrestling match, Greg was at GWO Headquarters in New York. The doctor had ordered an x-ray and an MRI of Greg's knee, and he was examining them carefully. The GWO had its own doctor. He was a good doctor, and Greg had been treated by him before. As good a doctor as he was, the GWO paid his salary, and sometimes he had bent to the wishes of the GWO, or even the wrestlers when it came to clearing wrestlers to return to the ring.

Greg was a little concerned about his knee injury, but he didn't think it was too serious. He had injured the same knee a year earlier. He thought it had healed sufficiently, but apparently not sufficiently enough. He couldn't afford to be out of wrestling now, especially not now. With the possibility of starring in a major movie, he needed to remain in the public eye. Even a short time away from wrestling could impact his career, either in wrestling or as an aspiring actor.

Greg had wanted to get into acting for quite some time now. His wrestling career wouldn't last forever, although he had known wrestlers to drag out their careers well past their prime. He knew a few wrestlers who had wrestled into their sixties. They had left the larger wrestling organizations and wrestled with very small regional independent organizations that paid very little. He didn't know if they did it because wrestling was so much in their blood that they couldn't stop or if they just couldn't think of anything else to do. Greg definitely didn't want to go that route, which was one of the reasons he really wanted to get into acting. He liked wrestling to a point, but it was hard work. He certainly didn't start at the top and knew he wouldn't end up at the top if he stayed in wrestling too long. Hunter Savage wasn't always his wrestling persona. He had started at the bottom. One of his previous wrestling personas was filling in for an injured wrestler who wore a mask, the *Wrestling Tornado*. The Wrestling Tornado had been injured during a match, and since Greg was the same height and build, he was asked to wear the mask and assume that role until the injured wrestler recuperated. He had a few other personas until he landed on his current one, Hunter Savage. Once he adopted his current persona, he quickly rose through the ranks, becoming world wrestling champion for the first time when he was twenty-five years old. He had been the world wrestling champion a total of three times, his most recent reign being the longest at three years. He figured he could carry off his current persona for another twelve years until he aged out of being a believable playboy. Twelve years was a long time, definitely longer than he wanted to remain in wrestling. He just had to land this acting role for which he auditioned.

As Greg waited for the doctor to finish studying the x-ray, thoughts of his injury and its possible implications began to invade Greg's mind once more, which made him nervous, and he began to fidget with his fingers, a nervous compulsion he had developed in his teens. Finally, the doctor turned around, facing him.

"Greg, you have a Medial Collateral Ligament tear."

"I've had that before," lamented Greg.

"Well, as the old doctor joke goes, you have it again." The doctor looked at Greg. The doctor had a dry sense of humor, and Greg assumed that the doctor was waiting for a chuckle, but Greg didn't laugh. "That's why I never went into comedy," continued the doctor. The doctor held up an older image from Greg's file and compared it to the new one. "It was milder before, but it's still relatively minor. Although you could wrestle sooner, I would generally recommend a structured rehabilitation program for four weeks. Since you seem prone to this injury, I would prefer that you avoid wrestling for eight weeks, just to be on the safe side and to avoid possible surgery if you have a major tear."

"Doc, you know my contract is up on December 31st, and I have a possible movie role. I really need to be on top of my game now more than ever."

"You've been a world champion three times, and you're currently the longest reigning champion in the history of the organization. Surely that counts as something if you negotiate your contract."

"Not when it comes to renegotiation," appealed Greg.

"The wear and tear on your body, plus the fact that you've had this injury before, makes it more likely that it will be much more serious in the future if you don't take the time to take care of it now. If you end up with a major tear it would probably require surgery, which would put you out of wrestling for at least six months."

"What's the best you can do?" From Greg's knowledge of the doctor, he knew that if he persisted, the doctor would more than likely give in.

"I really shouldn't, but I'll recommend at least one week of rehabilitation before I release you to wrestle," submitted the doctor.

"You're the best, doc."

"You won't be saying that if this turns into something worse. You can go. I need to finish up your file on the computer. I'll prescribe an anti-inflammatory medication. If you have any pain, just take some acetaminophen."

Escape was all Greg could think of as he exited the doctor's office, but in the waiting room, he recognized a wrestler he had not seen in a long time. Ric Suave, a former world champion, waited to see the doctor. Greg patterned a lot of his wrestling persona after Ric, who now had to be at least in his early to mid-fifties and was a shadow of his former glory. Twenty years ago, on television and at matches, Ric was over-the-top in his wrestling persona. The man sitting in the chair was far from that. Of course, Greg knew better than anyone that one's wrestling persona could be nothing like one's real self. Still, Ric appeared to be the loneliest, most depressed-looking person that Greg could have conjured up in his mind.

"Ric!" called out Greg as he limped over to shake his hand. "I heard you were coming back to the GWO from another organization. You're not injured already, are you?"

"No. Just have to get clearance to wrestle."

Both men were quiet after Ric's comment. Greg was unsure of what to say at this point; Ric certainly wasn't furthering the conversation. Finally, Greg said the only thing he could think of. "Man, I looked up to you. You were a great world champion."

That seemed to loosen Ric's tongue. "Wrestling's in my blood, but it takes a toll. Six times world champion, four times divorced, and three children I'm estranged from who won't have anything to do with me because I was never there for them. Now, nobody remembers my past glory. I mainly serve as a fall guy to younger wrestlers."

Greg had intended what he said to be a compliment. He didn't know if Ric took it that way or as a stinging reminder of who he no longer was. And the response that Ric gave simultaneously chilled Greg to the bone while sending a red-hot poker to his head that physically made him light-headed. It was his worst fear. Family was let down, and perhaps even worse sounding to Greg was the fact that this was what Greg's life could turn into if he didn't secure the movie role. What would he do if his physique, popularity, and personality failed him? The answer was before his eyes. Greg wanted to force the conversation to a more positive note. "But you had a great ride."

"The thing about rides," Ric stated slowly, "is that they end sooner than you expect. And if you don't have anyone waiting for you when they're over, what do you have? Take my advice, Greg. Don't let all the traveling do to you what it did to me. When you don't have a family, that's when you realize how important family really is."

When you never have a family. Greg repeated the statement in his mind. He never truly had a family. Well, he did, but he had never experienced what one says having a family feels like. Not with his parents. Not even with Stephanie and Austin. The whole concept seemed foreign to him. If you couldn't make yourself happy, then who else could? And if at some point you couldn't make yourself happy ... well that was what Greg wanted to put out of his mind. What do you do when your life betrays you? He certainly didn't want to entertain the notion.

Greg's thoughts were interrupted by the sound of an opening door behind him. The doctor was walking out of his office to take Ric back. Before Greg realized it, he asked, "Hey doc! Would you mind changing that to four weeks out, and can you recommend someone for physical rehabilitation in the Cincinnati area?"

The doctor's face lit up, as if no one in the wrestling world had ever asked for an extension on their time out. In fact, he seemed ecstatic. "Glad you changed your mind! You won't be sorry. I'll find someone in the Cincinnati area and text you the information."

He debated for several hours whether he should call Stephanie with the news that he would watch Austin. Her parents would probably be upset hearing the news at the last minute, but he was on medical release, and now was as good a time as any to spend with Austin. She seemed surprised to hear from him the same day. "Hey, Steph. I'll watch Austin while you're away." Greg hung up the phone and wondered if he had made the correct decision. Well, it was done now. He had not spent that much time with Austin since Austin was around two years old. A sudden wave of regret washed over Greg. He had forgotten what time of the year it was. It was close to

Christmas, Greg's least favorite time of the year. No doubt, Austin would want to do something to get ready for Christmas … or would he? Greg didn't know if Austin was that much into Christmas or not. Hopefully, he wouldn't be, but if he was … well, Greg was confident that he could come up with lots of other fun things to do with Austin. Besides, Stephanie would probably want to do those things once she returned. As long as he wasn't outside building a snowman, baking Christmas Cookies, or decorating a tree. Maybe they could go to a football game, or maybe he could take Austin to one of GWO's weekly wrestling events. He'd think of something.

Stephanie knew Austin would be doing his homework as she walked upstairs to his room. She wondered if she should wait until the morning to tell Austin so that Austin wouldn't be so excited that he wouldn't go to sleep. Of course, the morning was always busy, and it would be difficult to tell him, and perhaps he would need some time to process it before going to school. She really needed to call her parents tonight and inform them, and there was the chance that Austin would overhear. Perhaps now was the best time after all. She only hoped that Greg wouldn't change his mind. That would devastate Austin, and her parents wouldn't be too happy either to have planned, disrupt those plans, and then plan again.

Austin kept the door to his room open. He hadn't yet reached those years where he demanded privacy. They would come soon enough, and then she would receive payment in full for having done that with her parents. She walked into his room, which was like a shrine to Hunter Savage. Posters of Hunter Savage covered the walls. Austin was doing his homework, which was a good sign.

Stephanie wasn't sure how to approach the subject other than the direct route. "Austin, honey. Your dad is going to come watch you instead of your grandparents while I'm away at training."

Austin dropped his pencil, and his eyes widened. Stephanie could see the excitement bubble up from the bottom all the way to the top and into his forehead. "Really? He'll be here the whole time?" Austin squirmed in his seat, unable to contain his excitement.

"He really will."

A wistful, pensive look suddenly appeared on Austin's face, which automatically worried Stephanie.

"What's wrong, honey?"

"I wish you could stay here too. You promised that we would do all kinds of Christmas things."

"Your dad's not much into Christmas." It was all Stephanie could do to keep from sighing.

"Why not?" asked Austin inquisitively. He continued before Stephanie could answer, which was, she thought, because she didn't know how to answer the question in a way that Austin would understand. Although she knew his rationale, she didn't fully understand it herself. "Getting ready for Christmas is the only thing I've had to look forward to since we moved here. We were going to try some new things since it's colder here than in Florida. Will you ask him to do Christmas things with me? Please?"

Austin's pleading nearly broke her heart. She'd have to find a way to convince him. "I'll tell him."

Stephanie was thinking how to convince her stubborn ex-husband to capitulate to Austin's wishes. Since when was she able to convince her stubborn ex-husband of anything? And since she would be away, how could she hold him to any promises? Suddenly, a thought sprang into her head as if by magic. She smiled. Perhaps it would work. She hurried downstairs and grabbed her phone. Searching through her contacts, she found the number she was looking for and pressed her finger to the number.

The phone rang, and then she heard, "hello."

"Hi, Jennifer. I've got a big favor to ask."

A Porsche or an SUV

Greg stood at the airport rental car office with his luggage after the short two-hour flight from JFK to the Cincinnati/Northern Kentucky International Airport. He rarely had the opportunity to drive anymore, and he was going to take full advantage of that opportunity now. The rental car company had to get the car he requested from another agency since they didn't keep that car there, which cost him plenty extra. He completed the necessary information at the desk and eagerly went to pick up his car. There, waiting for him, was a two-door Porsche Boxster convertible with a manual transmission.

It had been easy to pick out. His eyes were drawn almost instantly to the sleek, aerodynamic design of the car. He could feel the German engineering as soon as he grasped the door handle. He was careful to avoid putting too much strain on his knee as he lowered himself behind the wheel, sighing as he sank into the leather seats. He sat behind the wheel for a few minutes simply admiring the car's beauty and luxury. "I could get used to this," he said aloud. He turned the key and the engine roared to life with a hungry growl, eager to get on the road. Greg felt the power surge through him, almost as if he were an extension of the car.

Even though the weather was cold, Greg rode with the top down. The wind tousled his hair. There was no brushing his hand through his hair as he did when he was in his wrestling persona of Hunter Savage. The car responded with such precision to his steering that he wished he could drive for hours on an open road; it was pure, unadulterated joy that ended way too soon to suit him.

When he pulled into the driveway of Stephanie's house, he noticed the uninspiring SUV that was parked there. He didn't even want to park the Porsche beside of it. He certainly hoped he wouldn't have to drive the thing while he was here. Before getting out of the car, Greg used the rearview mirror to try to comb his disheveled hair into a reasonable semblance of his hairstyle. He brushed his hands through his hair, à la Hunter Savage, and adjusted his sunglasses before reluctantly climbing out of the car. He had forgotten about his knee, but it reminded him of its injury when he got out of the car. He would have to be more careful in the future.

With suitcase in hand, he walked up and rang the doorbell to Stephanie's house. It was a nice-looking house in a quaint neighborhood. Although he was born and grew up in the Cincinnati area, he had not spent much time in this particular suburb.

Stephanie opened the door, and her eyes went immediately to the Porsche parked next to her SUV. "What is that?"

Greg mimicked Stephanie since she had not greeted him. "Why hello, Greg. It's good to see you. Hi, Steph. It's good to see you too. Please come in. Thank you. I don't mind if I do." Greg flashed a smile after the one-sided greeting exchange.

Stephanie smiled and shook her head. "Hello, Greg. It is good to see you. I was just surprised to see that car parked in my driveway. I would have picked you up from the airport, you know. And you could have used my car. You didn't have to rent one that is obviously very expensive."

"That car is a Porsche Boxster convertible. That thing you're driving isn't exactly my idea of a car the World

Wrestling Champion should be driving. You should feel how it drives. I'll let you try it."

"Your rental car isn't exactly my idea of a car a parent with a nine-year old should be driving, and you'll probably agree with me once Austin scatters all of his belongings all over it and puts his dirty, sticky hands all over it. By then, you'll be begging to drive my SUV. Besides, I don't think the Porsche is a car you should drive around with our son. You can drive my SUV." Stephanie paused to let what she had said sink in. "But I will take you up on your offer to let me drive it," she said with a smile to let Greg know that there were no hard feelings.

Greg flashed a smile. He always had a way of disarming her with his charm, even for an ex-husband. Suddenly, Stehanie became aware of her appearance. Although she was no longer in love with Greg, she still didn't want to appear as she was now, unshowered, no makeup, and unflattering clothes. "Excuse my appearance, I should have made myself a little more presentable."

"Nonsense. You look good no matter what."

"You're a good actor. Maybe you'll get that part after all." She sprinted up a few steps. "I'm glad you're here, and Austin will be really excited to see you. You can stay in the guest bedroom upstairs." She noticed Greg's knee. "Are you able to walk up the stairs?"

"Yeah. My knee is a little tender yet, but it'll be ok."

"At least let me carry your suitcase." Stephanie looked around to see if he had any other luggage. "Is that all you brought?"

"Thanks, Steph. Yes. That's it. You know with all the traveling I do, I learned to pack light. As soon as I unpack, I'm going to go to the school to talk with Austin's teacher."

"I've already spoken with her."

"You said that you hoped I could help bring him out of his shell."

"Yes ... but ... never mind. You should be able to catch her during her planning period." What's the use, thought Stephanie. He just never listens.

"Where is Austin's school exactly?"

"Let me write everything down for you." She went to an end table to fetch a pen and pad. "I'll write the name of the school, and you can use your GPS to get there. Austin's teacher's name is Ms. Bell. She teaches fourth grade social studies and language arts. You'll want to get there during the last period of the day. That's when she has her planning period." Stephanie observed Greg's blank face. "I'll write the bell schedule down for you too, so that you'll know when each period is. You'll have to check in at the office when you get there. I do have you listed as being able to see Austin and his teachers. Oh, Austin's math and science teacher is Helen Collins."

"Wow. That's a lot."

"I'm sure you can handle it. You travel from city to city all the time. But seeing as you have so much to remember, I'll pick up Austin from school."

"Good. That will give me the chance to drive the Porsche again."

Stephanie just shook her head. She smiled as she thought of one last dig on Greg. "By the way, those three flashy women who hang all over you on tv are not to set foot in this house."

"Very funny," deadpanned Greg. "I assume you are joking and that you know the women are just playing a part. Besides, I haven't dated anyone in as long as … Well, in as long as you haven't dated anyone."

Stephanie kept a blank expression on her face just to keep Greg guessing on the dating comment.

Biceps Bigger than Manners

Greg had been cleared at the office. The short, feisty, sixty-something-year-old woman in the office had put him through the ringer with security questions, security wanding, photo, and id check. He thought he was going to have to give his fingerprints to get past her. In his mind, he pictured her in a wrestling ring trouncing other wrestlers. He smiled at the thought. She had rattled off directions to Ms. Bell's classroom that Greg was now having difficulty following. He made a couple wrong turns but finally found the door with the name *Ms. Bell*.

The door was open, and Greg was about to knock when he noticed Ms. Bell working at her desk. He was struck by how pretty she was. Why had he not had teachers like that when he was in school? He knew you couldn't judge a book by its cover, but he sensed she was very down-to-earth, the girl next door type who was pretty but either didn't know it or didn't let it go to her head. The thought made Greg think of an old country music song called *She Don't Know She's Beautiful* sung by Sammy Kershaw. One of the lines in the song said something about the woman not knowing what all the fuss was about when told she was beautiful. Greg knocked on the door, and Ms. Bell looked up.

"Come in. May I help you?"

"Ms. Bell? I'm Greg Hunter, Austin's father. My ex-wife said our son, Austin, was having some trouble in school. Do you have time to talk?"

"Oh, please come in Mr. Hunter."

Greg walked in and went to sit at a desk in front of Ms. Bell's desk. He tried to sit but couldn't fit in the desk. He stood up and inspected the desk. Next, he awkwardly put his uninjured knee in the seat, but even it became stuck. Greg looked up and noticed an amused expression on Ms. Bell's face. "It's a little small." He could feel his face turning red from embarrassment.

She pointed to a chair and smiled. "You can sit in that chair. It's a little bigger. We have a tight budget here at the school. I wouldn't want you breaking a child's desk. We might not be able to replace it for a while."

"We break tables and chairs in my line of work all the time."

"We try not to do that here. Besides, your organization's budget is probably bigger than ours."

Greg went to the larger chair. It would have been big enough for an average-sized person, but Greg's muscular frame was still a little big for the chair. The chair creaked under his weight as he sat down awkwardly. Greg's face felt warm, and he thought that his face still must be red. Not a good first impression, he thought. He figured he had better start the conversation before he got any more embarrassed. "So, about Austin?"

"I was telling your ex-wife that Austin has been struggling with the other children. They don't believe that you're his father, and the children make fun of him. His grades are slipping as well."

"So, you're saying he's being bullied?" Greg noticed that his statement had caused a shocked expression on the teacher's face.

Ms. Bell stammered as she responded to Greg's accusation. "No ... he's not being bullied. It's just ..."

Greg interrupted before she could finish. "Isn't it your responsibility to stop the other children from making fun of him and to see that he gets more involved with his social interactions and with his schoolwork?"

"That's why I told your ex-wife and why I'm telling you. I'm not his parent. If you think it is so easy, why don't you come by tomorrow and observe?"

Greg could see that Ms. Bell's face was red now. She rose from her seat and walked to the door. Although the door was open, she opened it wider, and with wide eyes motioned with her head for him to leave.

Greg got up awkwardly from his chair. As he left, he almost ran into Helen Collins, who smiled giddily at him. They danced around each other, both trying to get by. Finally, they were able to get out of each other's way. Greg stole one last glance at Ms. Bell and saw her blow air out of her mouth in an exasperated manner. In the hallway, he could overhear part of the two teachers' conversation before he got out of earshot.

"Hi, Helen. Parents. Sometimes they make me wonder why I'm still a teacher."

"Who was that? He is so dreamy. Did you see his biceps?"

"That blow hard is Austin Hunter's father, and it's too bad his manners aren't as big as his biceps."

The Daily Special

Greg heard Stephanie's Ford Escape pull into the driveway, and he readied himself to see Austin. He never knew how Austin would react upon seeing him. So far, Austin had always been excited to see him. Hopefully, he would be today as well. At some point, Austin would probably not feel that way. Greg could not help thinking about Ric Suave's statement about his estrangement from his children, which sent a shudder through Greg's body. The shudder awakened a dull pain in Greg's knee.

Greg heard the front door open and footsteps running through the house. The footsteps found him in the kitchen. "Dad! I can't believe you're here." Austin ran to Greg and hugged him tightly. Stephanie entered the kitchen. "Mom said you're going to stay with me while she's in London."

"That's right, buddy. We'll do all kinds of fun stuff."

"Like decorate for Christmas while mom is away?"

"Well, maybe some other fun things. I'm not much on Christmassy things."

"Mom. You said you would talk with him."

"Greg, getting ready for Christmas is one of the few things that Austin has looked forward to since we moved here. Can't you put your feelings aside for him?"

"I don't want to take away what you usually do with him. Can't you do those things when you get back?" Greg hoped that would be enough to pull on Stephanie's heartstrings to end the matter.

"It will be too close to Christmas. Please, Greg. Just do it."

Greg was afraid that would be her answer; so, he tried Plan B. He turned to Austin. "With all the things I have planned, I bet you'll forget all about Christmas."

"Mom! Tell him."

Greg noticed Stephanie's frown. "I see you're still as stubborn as ever. Maybe you should try to be the world champion of that," she replied.

Greg thought about teasing Stephanie that she was already the world champion of that but thought better of it.

"Wouldn't you rather go to a football game? Or maybe we could go to one of the live wrestling events," offered Greg.

"Greg," interjected Stephanie in what Greg interpreted as an admonishing tone. "Look at me and listen to me. You need to make sure that Austin does his homework. Doing some Christmas activities will take less time than those big alternatives you have. Plus, going to those events as an observer is much different than participating in something yourself. I'm serious. Do some Christmas activities with Austin. He hasn't asked you for much. You can at least give him this."

Stephanie seemed adamant, and Greg felt somewhat scolded. No matter how hard he was trying, it didn't look as though he would get out of this.

"Now, I need to pack. My flight leaves early in the morning," added Stephanie.

"Don't you want to take a turn driving the Porsche?"

"Don't think you can charm your way out of this," declared Stephanie. "Why don't you make dinner?" Stephanie hesitated. "On second thought, I remember your cooking. Why don't you go pick up dinner?"

"Hey, I might have gotten a lot better since the last time you ate my cooking." He noticed Stephanie looking at him incredulously. "Ok. I'll go pick something up."

"Can I come with you, dad?"

"Why don't you stay here and get a head start on your homework. After dinner, I'll help you." Greg thought about asking him to come along, but he didn't want Austin to expect too much from him. After all, in about three weeks, he would be heading out again. As he entertained these thoughts, a cloud of guilt settled over him. His conscience chastised him for even having such thoughts, but Austin would have to face the reality of him leaving again.

"Ok." Austin sounded a little dejected.

Greg's knee was hurting some, and he was standing awkwardly to take some of the pressure off. He noticed Austin staring at his knee.

"How's your knee, dad?"

Greg rubbed the injured knee. "It's a little sore. The doctor found someone nearby who he recommended for physical therapy. So, during the day, I'll need to go to the physical therapist for a while."

"Just make sure your schedule allows you to get back in time to pick up Austin from school," warned Stephanie.

"Alright," Greg continued. "I'd better go pick up dinner." He went outside and got in the Porsche. I have no clue where to go, he thought. He pulled out his phone and found a diner nearby that had good ratings. He put the address into the GPS and was at the diner within a few minutes. Greg parked the car, and he wasn't thinking about his knee as he climbed out and wrenched his body, sending a shooting pain to his knee.

Greg hobbled inside the diner. It was quaint looking. He grabbed a menu but noticed the daily specials on a board. He made his way to the register where the worker appeared to be about eighteen years old or early twenties at most. The worker was absorbed with something on his phone and didn't notice Greg until Greg cleared his throat, startling the young man. The guy just stared at Greg. This diner must be desperate for workers, thought Greg. Finally, Greg spoke since the young man wasn't going to. "I'll take three daily specials please."

The guy seemed harried. "Will that be for here or to go?"

Greg looked around as if seeing if anyone else was with him. "I know I'm a big guy, but I'm not going to eat that many meals myself."

The worker looked questioningly at Greg.

"To go," said Greg. Where do they hire these people, he wondered?

The worker grabbed an order pad, wrote down the order and took it to the window that opened into the kitchen. The cook just shook his head and took the order ticket.

Greg's knee was feeling a little better now, and he walked over to an end seat at the counter and plopped down to wait for his order. He heard the door open but didn't look around.

Jennifer Bell walked into the diner to pick up her order. She proceeded to the register to where the worker was intently looking at his phone. "I have a call-in for Jennifer Bell."

Greg heard the name and the voice he had heard earlier that day. He took a quick glance toward the register. Sure enough, it was Ms. Bell. He quickly turned back around, hoping that she would not see him. Since they were the only two customers in the diner, the hope would probably be short lived. He turned his back to her and picked up a menu, which he held close to his face. He scrunched up his body to try to make himself appear smaller. As if that won't attract attention, he said to himself sarcastically.

The worker anxiously skimmed through orders. "Uh, I'm sorry. We must have lost the order."

There is no *we*, thought Greg. **You** lost the order, buddy. Of that, he was sure.

"It was for two daily specials."

Sounds as though she has a boyfriend, thought Greg.

"I'm sorry," replied the young man. "We're all out. I just took an order for the last one."

"Carol is going to be so upset," Jennifer mumbled.

"What was that?" the man asked. Jennifer sighed. "Ok. I guess I'll take two Cobb Salads."

"Order up," came a call from the cook. The worker strolled over to the counter, picked up the order and motioned to Greg. "Sir, your order is ready."

There's no getting around this, thought Greg as he sidled to the register. When Jennifer spotted him, Greg observed her put two and two together. Although he couldn't read her mind, he could tell from her face what she was thinking.

"Oh, so you're the one who took the last daily special after I had called it in."

The man handed Greg his order.

"I'm sorry. I didn't know. I don't think my son eats salad, but we could trade some of the meals."

Jennifer huffed. "No. Never mind."

"Order up," came the cry again from the cook.

The worker strolled over and picked up the salads while Jennifer just stared at Greg. "Your order is ready," the man said, handing the two salads to Jennifer.

Both Jennifer and Greg turned to leave at the same time. Greg's knee buckled slightly, and he stumbled, accidentally knocking the bag out of Jennifer's hand. The bag fell to the floor, spilling the contents of the salads onto the floor.

Greg was both horrified and embarrassed. He knew he had been abrupt and rude earlier toward the teacher, and this would certainly make her think even worse of him. "It was an accident. Let me pay for those."

"I'll take care of it. We don't need any more disasters today. Just get the meals home before they get cold."

Greg was hesitant. He didn't want to make matters worse, which could easily happen if he stayed and tried to help. Maybe the best thing was to leave and try to preserve any dignity he had remaining. With that decision made, he walked toward the door and felt Jennifer's stare bore a hole through him.

Jennifer stared at Greg as he walked to the door and out of the diner. Then, she turned to the worker and stated in her most authoritative teacher's voice, "I need two more Cobb Salads, and I'm not paying extra."

"Yes, ma'am," gulped the worker. Now he's alert, thought Jennifer.

Dufus Dads and Meddling Moms

When Jennifer arrived home, she saw Carol's car in the driveway. Carol had a key and could let herself in. Jennifer always looked forward to this time with her sister. Usually, the two sisters met at least once a week. It had become a tradition to meet at Jennifer's house with Jennifer picking up food from the diner. Sometimes, their parents would join them, but usually their parents would come over sometime during the weekend.

The two sisters had outgrown the normal childhood sibling rivalry and were very close. Oh, they would still take shots at one another on occasion, but they were more playful taps than the hard jabs of early adolescence. Jennifer was the older of the two by five years, and they were the only two children their parents had. They weren't exactly opposites but were close to it. Jennifer was more on the shy side whereas Carol was definitely extroverted. Jennifer liked to have and follow a plan; Carol was a free spirit. Jennifer was into traditions and didn't prefer change; Carol was adaptable.

Opening the front door required a balancing act. Not only was Jennifer carrying two salads but also her bag with all of her students' work to review along with props from the play that she needed to repair or spruce up.

"Is this your idea of a workout?" exclaimed Carol as Jennifer stumbled through the doorway.

The bags began slipping in Jennifer's hands. "A little help would be appreciated!"

Carol grabbed the bags with the salads. The daily special was meatloaf, and Jennifer knew she was expecting that. She could almost see Carol's mouth watering. Carol pointed her nose in the air and sniffed. The thought of a bloodhound came into Jennifer's mind at the sight. On second thought, a bloodhound would be sniffing the ground if she wanted to be precise about it.

"I have been waiting for meatloaf all day. It's almost all I've thought about." Carol sniffed the air again. "Wait, I don't smell meatloaf."

"It's a long story, but I had to get Cobb Salads. I'm sorry our dinner date is ruined."

"Ah. It's no biggie," declared Carol as she waived her hand to doubly indicate that it was not a problem. "I should eat more salads anyway, especially going into this time of the year with all of the parties and sweets."

Typical Carol. She was able to let almost anything roll off her like water off a duck's back. Jennifer wished she were more like Carol in that regard. Instead, she was almost the opposite.

"What happened anyway?"

Jennifer let out a "hmph" and began to tell the story talking faster as she went. "The diner lost my order, and one of my student's dufus dads got the last of the daily specials. Then he bumped into me on the way out and knocked lettuce all over the floor. He just gaped at me and sashayed out without offering to help. They had to make two more. At least they didn't charge me again for them. And if all that wasn't enough, he had come by the school earlier and accused me of letting other kids bully his son."

"That was rude."

"What would you expect from a professional wrestler?"

"Dufus Dad is a professional wrestler? Who is it? Stuart, you know the guy I used to date, was really into wrestling. So, I'm familiar with a lot of them, unless it's a small independent organization."

There she goes, thought Jennifer. I'd better tell her the name before she gets into a long, drawn-out story. If she had actually gotten the meatloaf, it would be cold by the time Carol finished her story. Perhaps Carol was the one who should be a writer. "The name he wrestles under is Hunter Savage."

"Hunter Savage! He's the world champion. He was like Stuart's favorite. Stuart had some of his collectibles. I think I still have a shirt Stuart let me borrow that has Hunter Savage on it."

"Don't let me see you wearing it." Jennifer paused. "And to think, I promised Stephanie … well, never mind."

"Wait a minute. Your neighbor, Stephanie, was married to Hunter Savage? What did you promise her? Out with it. You can't say and not say."

Her sister was like a dog with a bone. She would keep at it until Jennifer acquiesced. Jennifer laughed to herself; she always seemed to be comparing her sister to a dog.

"Alright! Apparently, Greg Hunter, who is Stephanie's ex-husband, and whose son Austin is in my class, doesn't like Christmas. One of the things that Austin has been looking forward to is Christmas. Austin has been having a difficult time in school; so, I can see why he is looking forward to something to occupy his mind. Anyway, Greg is going to watch Austin while Stephanie is away for something at work. Although she told Greg to do some Christmas things with Austin, she thinks that with her gone, he'll just skip the Christmas activities altogether. So, Stephanie asked me to keep an eye on them and coax Greg into doing things."

"You're going to love that," stated Carol.

A look of confusion spread over Jennifer's face. "Why do you say that?"

"Come on, sis. You're like Ms. Christmas. I wish I could watch this. It will be like the Ghost of Christmas Future versus Ebenezer Scrooge." Carol began laughing hysterically.

"What are you laughing about?"

"Hunter Savage is a wrestler, and I just got this image in my mind of you two in a wrestling ring as the Ghost of Christmas Future and Ebenezer Scrooge grappling to see who would win. My money is on you, by the way, but I do feel a little sorry for him."

"Why is that?"

"Just because you have to celebrate every Christmas the same way every year for as long as you can remember doesn't mean that everyone else does."

There was some truth in what Carol said. Those traditions had been instilled in her by rote memory. She had been taught certain traditions in the same way she had been taught subtraction or long division ... by doing them over and over. Carol had been taught the same traditions though, yet she wasn't adverse to change at all. Jennifer's thoughts were interrupted by Carol's continued ramblings.

"You should have been the one with the Christmas name. I've had to live with the name, Carol Bell, my whole life. Every time someone says my name, I expect the *Hallelujah Chorus* to break out."

Jennifer flashed a big smile. "I was thinking more *Carol of the Bells*!"

"Ha ha." If I had a …" Carol hesitated. "I started to say dime, but if I had a bell for every time someone said that to me, I could supply a handbell set to every choir in the world."

"Let's not exaggerate, maybe every choir in the greater Cincinnati area," proposed Jennifer.

"Let's compromise. Every choir in the United States," countered Carol.

"Every choir in Ohio."

"What are we, in elementary school?" exclaimed Carol.

"Well, I do teach elementary school. I guess it wears off on me." Their exchange reminded Jennifer of when they were much younger. They used to have those back and forths a lot, and they drove their parents crazy every time.

They ate in silence, except for the crunching of lettuce and carrots. It was a good thing they had salads instead of meatloaf; it would have been cold by now. Eating was about the only time Carol didn't talk. She had been broken of that habit by their mom a long time ago.

"Here. Give me your plate. I'll do the dishes." Carol grabbed both empty salad containers, traipsed over to the trash can and threw them in.

"You always did get the easy jobs," chided Jennifer.

"Whatever!" Carol replied, rolling her eyes the way she did when she was a teenager.

"Well, you've at least cheered me up from today's episodes with dufus dad."

Carol lifted her chin and put her index finger to the side of her forehead, a funny sight, but also an indication that Carol was in deep thought, which was usually a sign of trouble.

"Hunter Savage is rather nice looking," revealed Carol finally.

"Oh, no. I know what you're about to say. You're as meddlesome as mom."

"Well, you had the same boyfriend forever until last year. You haven't had to experience her always trying to set you up with a friend of a friend's cousin until just recently."

"She's certainly tried to make up for lost time this past year." That comment had been said in jest with a smile on her face, but suddenly Jennifer grew melancholy. It was though hands were reaching up and pulling her into a pit of darkness.

Carol apparently noticed the shift in Jennifer's demeanor. "Don't let Steve get you down. Be glad you're rid of him."

I haven't felt like dating anyone since Steve broke up with me. We dated for probably fourteen years, but he was rarely with me because of this or that, work mostly. In all that time, he wouldn't marry me. Yet, to advance his career, he leaves me and becomes engaged within a few months. You, mom, and dad knew the type of person he was all along, but I couldn't see it."

"People never see things plainly with themselves."

"I never want to fall for anyone like that again. Perhaps it's best to not date anyone at all."

"Well, I'm not going to let you stay all sad and mopey," replied Carol. "Since you don't trust yourself, I think you should let mom pick out a boyfriend for you."

Jennifer had been on the verge of tears, but suddenly she laughed through them. "You can't be serious."

"You might as well let her pick one out for you. Nothing's going to stop her until you walk down the aisle, and then she'll turn her attention to me."

"But you already have a boyfriend," remarked Jennifer.

"She'd just hound him to marry me. Then he would break up with me, and then I'd be just like you." Carol wore a smart alecky smile as if she had won a major argument. Carol got up and poured two glasses of wine. She handed one to Jennifer.

"Are we toasting to something?" asked Jennifer, who was now in a much better mood.

"Yes. To dufus dads and meddling moms!"

Teacher Mode

The feisty gatekeeper in the school office had been a pussycat today. Greg wanted to believe that his charm was what led to her change in temperament, but he had flashed that same charm the previous day. Maybe it took two doses of his charm for some people.

Today, he dressed more casually than he had yesterday. He wore his six-hundred-dollar sunglasses. Although he was inside, he had grown accustomed to wearing them. He was wearing jeans and one of his collectible T-shirts. The back of the T-shirt displayed the name *Hunter Savage*. Underneath his name were the backs of five playing cards. *Global Wrestling Organization* was displayed under the cards. The front of his T-shirt showed the five playing cards with the world championship belt on the face of each. Above the playing cards was the phrase, *The Best Player in the Game*. The T-shirt was tight-fitting. Perhaps that was the reason, rather than his charm, that the woman in the office was nicer to him today.

At first, he went unnoticed, almost as if he were invisible, as he wended down the crowded school hallway. Soon, however, all the children began to stare and whisper to each other. Then they started talking and pointing excitedly. Before he knew it, he was mobbed by fourth and fifth graders before he could get to the classroom. It appeared children recognized him more readily than adults. He finally made his way inside Ms. Bell's classroom. He closed the door, but children were looking through the window, and occasional thumping sounds could be heard as children were pressed against the door. He was a little flustered by the crowd of kids, but he was intact. Only his sunglasses were slightly ajar, but he quickly adjusted them.

Greg fixed his gaze on Ms. Bell, whose mouth was markedly wide open. Obviously, she must have thought he wouldn't show up. He scanned the room full of students and noticed that the boys' jaws had dropped as well. Austin scrambled out of his seat and ran up to his dad. They gave each other a fist bump, and Austin turned around toward the class and gave the boys an *I told you so* smile.

Greg was surprised at how quickly Ms. Bell gathered her wits and composure, no doubt a necessity for an elementary school teacher.

"Good afternoon, Mr. Hunter. We were just getting ready to start our history lesson about Alexander the Great. Perhaps you would like to share what you know about him with the children."

Greg was completely surprised and caught off guard by Ms. Bell's invitation. This wasn't a wrestling ring. He was in her territory now. He was hesitant as to what to do next, but something snapped him into focus, and he imagined that Ms. Bell was now surprised at how quickly he composed himself. The composure was short-lived, however. He turned an empty desk around at the front of the class to face the kids and awkwardly tried to sit in it. The children burst into laughter at the site of his 6 ft 3 in, 255-pound frame trying to fit into the tiny desk. He turned to face Ms. Bell, who was pointing, just as she had the day previously, to the larger chair next to her desk. Greg mustered his confidence and sauntered over to the chair. He turned the chair so that the back was facing the students and sat down, resting his arms on top of the back of the chair. Once again composed, the showman side of his wrestling persona took over.

"Actually, my middle name is Alexander, and when I was in school, I was a little on the shy and nerdy side, and everyone always picked on me."

By providing that statement, he hadn't realized that he set up Ms. Bell perfectly.

"You mean your teacher didn't stop the kids from bullying you?"

Greg smiled slyly as he remembered yesterday's conversation. *Touché*, he thought to himself, but he continued undeterred.

"The kids would call me *Alexaaaaander* in a mocking voice."

One of the boys in the class raised his arm.

Greg pointed to the boy. "Yes?"

"Did you beat them up?" quizzed the boy innocently.

"I stood up to the main one after school." He had hopefully redirected the question so that he did not have to give the actual outcome of what had happened when he stood up for himself.

A girl in the class interrupted. "Mr. Savage …, I mean Mr. Hunter, what happened?"

Greg answered without missing a beat. "The next day, I came to school with a black eye!"

The class burst into laughter once more. Greg casually cast a glance over to Ms. Bell, who was smiling. The humor in her eyes made them twinkle, and Greg found turning his attention back to the students difficult.

Greg continued. "But I didn't let that stop me. I told them there were important people named Alexander who changed the world. Alexander the Great conquered much of the world. By the age of thirty, he had one of the largest empires in the world, and when he died it took four generals to try to take his place. Then there was Alexander Graham Bell whom it took years to invent the telephone, and where would you be without your smartphones. He might be an ancestor of your teacher, Ms. Bell."

The children laughed, and Ms. Bell smiled. Greg was temporarily stymied at how beautiful Ms. Bell appeared when she smiled. At least he seemed to fare better with her today than yesterday. Hopefully, his charm would get him back on even ground with her. He continued before he lost himself in her beautiful smile. "Alexander Graham Bell made it a point not to give up, and he said that the only difference between success and failure was the ability to take action. The point is not to give up, to be yourself no matter the consequences, and to not let people making fun of you stand in your way from doing something worthwhile. It took me years to win a championship, but I never gave up. But let's get back to Alexander the Great. In one battle, Alexander came up against an army with 200 elephants, but he quickly adapted."

Greg had been talking for most of the period when the bell rang. The children quickly rushed out of the classroom, excitedly chatting about Hunter Savage as they headed for the last class of the day. Greg remembered that this was now Ms. Bell's planning period. He stood up from the chair to leave, but he didn't want to leave Ms. Bell's presence. Something drew him to her. He hadn't remembered being this intoxicated by anyone previously. He feigned stretching while he thought what to do or say next. Fortunately, Jennifer began some small talk.

"I bet you're stiff after sitting that way for the entire period."

"Yeah. I'm not used to sitting much."

"I'm sorry I put you on the spot." Jennifer's face squinted as if pained, and she smiled hesitantly and apologetically. "I hate to admit that I was trying to get back at you for what you said yesterday, and for taking the last two specials and for knocking my salads on the floor."

"That's ok. I deserved it, and your timing was spot on. And you were right; a teacher is not a parent. Also, I should have been more thoughtful last night in the diner."

Greg noticed a wave of relaxation wash over Jennifer at her realization that he wasn't upset. Her shoulders relaxed, and her conversation flowed much more easily.

"You did a great job. You made the lesson entertaining and involved them."

"If there is one thing I know, it's entertainment." Greg tossed his head back and ran his hand through his hair as if he were doing a wrestling interview.

Jennifer laughed and shook her head at his showy masquerade.

"You know a lot more than that. Did you ever think about being a teacher? You've got a knack for it."

Greg grew more serious at her compliments and question. "I majored in history in college, and I thought about teaching, but wrestling took over."

"So, tell me why you like wrestling, and tell me one thing I don't know about it."

"Nicely done," complimented Greg. "You slipped so naturally into teacher mode."

Jennifer laughed, and Greg became more intoxicated with each infectious laugh.

"I suppose I did. Sorry. It's a hard habit to break. Please forget that I asked."

"I would be a pretty poor student if I didn't answer the teacher's question. I like the way you asked the question. Often people ask if I like wrestling. You asked why I liked wrestling."

"Well, just asking if you like something will generally prompt a one-word response. To get people talking and to assess their communication and critical thinking, one has to ask questions in different ways." Jennifer stopped suddenly and blushed. "I'm sorry; I did it again."

Greg's arm made a slicing motion through the air as he responded. "Yep. Straight to teacher mode."

Jennifer smiled. "You're just buying time until you can think of an answer, aren't you?"

"Totally buying time." Greg was amazed at how at ease he felt with Ms. Bell.

"Quit stalling, buster," replied Jennifer jovially.

Greg struggled as he tried to answer. "I guess I like wrestling as a means of relaxation."

Jennifer eyed him questioningly, but she didn't make a comment. He wished she had, but she was a good teacher. She was forcing him to explain what he meant.

"Most people see me as a big extrovert, but I'm probably more introverted than extroverted. Wrestling allows me to put on a different persona, to act. I can be someone I'm not, someone I might be afraid to be normally. When I get into that persona, it's intoxicating, and it provides an outlet for all of the built-up energy or negative emotions I have."

Jennifer looked at Greg as if she were studying him, looking inside to see the real him. "You're right, I would never believe you to be an introvert. I'm not sure I believe it now. You're so at ease being the center of attention."

"I don't often reflect. Maybe I don't even know myself. I could have given a completely incorrect analysis of myself."

"I think there is at least some truth there or you wouldn't have said it."

Opening up to someone he barely knew was like standing in a spotlight. All of his insecurities were laid bare for her examination. The sensation was akin to being emotionally naked, and the experience both exhilarated and unnerved him. He didn't think he could be this open with anyone. Before he thought too much about what he had said, he hurriedly rushed to answer the other question that Ms. Bell had asked. "Ok, so, you want me to tell you something you don't know about wrestling." He pondered for a moment about what to say.

Jennifer eagerly leaned in as if awaiting him to tell her the meaning of life.

"Wrestlers are generally either babyfaces or heels."

Greg was amused at the way Jennifer scrunched her eyebrows together, clearly not comprehending his statement. "A babyface is the good guy, and the heel is the bad guy."

"So, you're a babyface."

Greg couldn't tell if she was asking a question or simply making a statement. If it was a statement, he was surprised that she would think he was a good guy after the way he had acted toward her yesterday. "Actually, I'm a heel at the moment, but I have been a babyface before. Lots of fans like heels more than babyfaces. I act as though I have a chip on my shoulder. I brag. I'm self-absorbed. I cheat in the ring." Greg could almost tell what Jennifer was thinking. "As I said, I'm sorry for the way I acted yesterday."

"So, now you're a babyface?"

"You've made me see the light, and I've changed my ways," kidded Greg melodramatically.

"This is interesting. Tell me something else."

"Have you ever heard of kayfabe?"

"No. Who's she?" asked Jennifer.

"Not a name, Kay Fabe, but *kayfabe*. Kayfabe refers to presenting professional wrestling as though it were real and unscripted rather than entertainment."

"Doesn't everyone know it's not real?" Jennifer looked up at him with an apologetic expression after uttering those words. Her big, beautiful eyes drew him in, and he was momentarily speechless.

"I'm sorry," apologized Jennifer. "I didn't mean to offend you."

Greg snapped back to the present and realized that he had almost forgotten to answer her. "No offense taken. Prior to 1989, wrestlers went to great lengths to portray professional wrestling as a real contest or fight. Don't get me wrong. Wrestling is physically demanding, and people get hurt." He patted his injured knee on the word, *hurt*. "I think it's as tough or tougher than football or other contact sports."

Greg and Jennifer continued talking for almost the entire period. Eventually, Jennifer noticed the clock on the wall. She stood up, and Greg realized how long they had been talking.

"I'm sorry, Ms. Bell, for taking up your time."

"No. I really enjoyed talking with you. I would stay longer but I need to go to the auditorium before the kids arrive. We're starting our Christmas play today. Greg walked with Ms. Bell as she headed to the door. "I spoke to Stephanie about Austin being in it as a way to help him interact with more kids. Do you know if he wants to be in it?"

"Stephanie and I spoke with him last night about it, and he reluctantly agreed to do it." Greg paused and remembered that he wanted to tell Ms. Bell something. "By the way, that was really sly of both you and Stephanie not to let me know that you two knew each other and live that close to each other."

"You didn't really give me a chance."

"That's fair."

"Well, in full honesty now, your wife asked me to keep an eye on you and to make sure you do Christmas with Austin."

"I suppose she told you I don't do Christmas."

"We'll see. They don't call me Ms. Christmas for nothing."

"Sounds like a challenge. I accept, and I usually win my challenges."

At that moment, Helen Collins swished into the classroom. Greg was amused at how giddy she acted at seeing him. "Hi, I'm Helen Collins. I didn't know you were a famous professional wrestler. I heard you are the world champion. I'm sort of a champion too, but not to the extent you are. I'm the teacher of the year for the school district." She put her hand on Greg's bicep. "My, you have strong biceps. I've never met anyone famous before." She batted her eyes flirtatiously. "Perhaps, you would like to go get some coffee with me after school."

"I was just going with Ms. Bell to her Christmas play she's working on with the kids. I want to watch Austin try out for the play." Greg noticed the disheartened look on Helen's face for a brief moment, but then she put a big smile on her face.

"I'm going to hold you to that coffee. Another time, then?"

Greg didn't answer as he walked out with Jennifer. "It's nice to see you again, Ms. Collins."

Helen remained in Jennifer's classroom. Greg heard a giggle as he was in the hallway. He could imagine her putting her hand over her smile as she let out the giggle.

Helen stuck her head out of the door and called loudly to Greg. "You can call me Helen."

Three People Won't Fit in a Porsche

Greg and Jennifer were in the back of the auditorium. All of the children who wanted to take part in the play were starting to file into the auditorium. They ran past Greg and Jennifer. Most of the kids looked back at Greg and did a double take as they ran past. More and more children came in and made their way up front.

"I'm sorry about Helen." Jennifer cringed as if she were the one who should be embarrassed.

"No worries, Ms. Bell. I'm used to that. I get it at every arena."

"By the way, you don't have to call me Ms. Bell. You can call me Jennifer."

"At least you didn't yell it so the whole school could hear like Helen did." Greg noticed a shy look on Jennifer's face. Maybe he was an extrovert after all. "Jennifer it is, as long as you call me Greg instead of Mr. Hunter."

Jennifer smiled. "Deal."

They shook hands, and Jennifer turned around and strode toward the stage. The touch of Jennifer's soft hand sent chills through Greg. He couldn't remember the last time that had happened or if it ever had.

All the children were up front, talking and running around. Jennifer shouted above the commotion. "Ok, everyone, we're going to assign parts."

Greg noticed a few other parents on the other side of the auditorium in the back, and he walked over and introduced himself. Either some of them knew him, or their children had already told them who he was. He didn't know how the children could have already told them who he was. News certainly did travel quickly. Those who knew of him seemed excited to meet him in person. The others had no clue who he was, although a few did ask where Stephanie was. Once he explained that he was watching Austin for a few weeks while Stephanie was away on a work assignment, those parents seemed to warm quickly to him.

One woman introduced herself as the mother of Tommy McElroy. Greg remembered Stephanie telling him that Austin was having some trouble with Tommy McElroy, and he was completely taken aback when the boy's mother asked if Austin could come over sometime. Greg agreed and hoped this was a good sign.

Greg talked with several of the parents during the rehearsal, but he noticed that his attention kept drifting toward the stage and Jennifer. He purposely tried to keep his focus on the person with whom he was talking but the chore was almost impossible, and his focus invariably turned back to Jennifer. On one occasion, a parent commented. "I'm sorry, Mr. Hunter. I should let you watch the rehearsal."

Greg politely apologized and thought that his face had probably turned red from embarrassment. "I'm just checking to make sure I don't miss Austin."

After about an hour, the rehearsal ended. Some of the children and parents took off quickly. Other parents were still talking with each other while their children waited impatiently to leave the school and get home to other activities. By this time, Greg had moved to the center of the auditorium, a few rows back from the stage. The auditorium seating was a little better than that in Jennifer's classroom, but Greg's muscular frame still extended over the armrests. Jennifer spotted him and walked over toward him. She still seemed as though she had a lot of energy. He wasn't sure why she wasn't exhausted at this point after dealing with children all day. He knew that he would have been.

"Everyone did well." Greg paused, mustering his courage. "Hey, would you like to go get something to eat with Austin and me?" He added quickly, "Austin doesn't trust my cooking yet. I'll buy. It's the least I can do for what happened at the diner last night." A rush of adolescent jitters made his palms sweaty and his heart race as though he were a teenager asking a girl on a date; he started fidgeting with his fingers and was expecting the worst but was pleasantly surprised by her answer.

"Since you put it that way, and since I promised Stephanie that I would keep an eye on you and Austin, I'd love to. Are you ready to go now?"

"Sure, but you can pick the place. Although I grew up in the area, it was in a different suburb of Cincinnati."

"I'll take you to my favorite spot."

"The diner?" Greg kidded. "Do you want to make sure you get the special tonight? I'll challenge anyone who tries to take the last one away from you."

"No. You can keep your title another night. This is a different place." Jennifer regarded him slyly. "You did say you were buying, right?"

"Uh-oh. I may be in trouble now."

"Don't worry. It's not expensive."

She lightly put her hand on his bicep, and he hoped she couldn't feel the tingling running through his arm. Helen's touch was annoying, a totally different response than the soft, light, genuine touch from Jennifer. Jennifer removed her hand, and Greg fretted inwardly, immediately missing the soft, comforting touch. This must be what a baby feels like when someone takes away its pacifier, he thought. He remembered that he had driven the Porsche, and three people wouldn't fit, but he was still disappointed when Jennifer suggested that they drive separately. Get over it, he told himself; it makes a lot more sense to drive separately than to drive back to the school to pick up a car. He was going to follow her, but she also gave him the address to the place in case they got separated.

It's a Long Story

The restaurant was a short ten-minute drive from the school. They were fortunate to find two parking places next to each other close to the restaurant. Greg thought that the restaurant was rather quaint looking on the outside, certainly more appealing than the diner, but it still had that small-town vibe.

As they got out of their respective cars, Jennifer commented on Greg's car. "That car certainly suits Hunter Savage, but I'm surprised that Stephanie is letting you drive Austin around in it. Although, it would look strange seeing the world wrestling champion driving an SUV."

"She did say it wasn't practical or safe for a child, and she sentenced me to driving her vehicle. I suppose I'll need to start driving it, especially since you're keeping an eye on us for Stephanie. Just do me a favor and don't tell her about this one time."

Jennifer smiled the kind of mischievous smile that Greg couldn't determine if she would overlook this one instance or if she would tell Stephanie anyway.

Greg strode ahead of Jennifer and held the door open for her. He glided into the restaurant behind her and was astounded by all of the Christmas decorations that already adorned the restaurant. The restaurant looked as though the North Pole had exploded inside it, sending twinkling lights, shiny decorations, and mechanized Christmas knick-knacks to every available space. "They really do Christmas up big in this restaurant."

"Oh, I love Christmas. Don't you?" she asked, looking at Greg.

"Dad doesn't like Christmas," interjected Austin in a dejected manner.

"I don't dislike Christmas," Greg added quickly. "It's just another day."

"Not disliking Christmas is not the same as liking it," replied Jennifer. "Why don't you like Christmas?

Greg started fidgeting with his fingers again. "It's … a long story.

The hostess showed them to a table, which fortunately didn't have as many decorations as those that emblazoned the booths. The hostess gave them each a menu, and a waiter quickly arrived and took their orders. Austin began playing on his phone.

Both Greg and Jennifer were quiet, and Greg was again reminded of two teenagers on a first date. Greg hoped that the conversation would flow as easily as it had earlier in Jennifer's classroom. He knew that it was dating protocol to focus on the other person rather than oneself. When he began a conversation though, he found himself falling into the trap he had hoped to avoid. "Walking into that auditorium with all of those kids running around and playing reminded me of a wrestling match. I don't think I could have ever gotten them organized." Recognizing his faux pas, he quickly tried to divert the focus onto Jennifer. "So, I've never seen the Christmas play you're directing. Where did you find it?"

"Oh, I wrote it myself. It's not much, but I wanted to do something different this year. It's sort of a cross between *A Christmas Carol* and *It's a Wonderful Life.*"

"You wrote it yourself!" Greg was impressed and wondered how she had found the time and the energy to do something extra beyond teaching.

Jennifer reached into the bag she had brought in and pulled out a manuscript as though he didn't believe her. She handed it over to him.

"Wow, Jen. That's wonderful." Greg noticed that Jennifer stared at him somewhat surprised when he called her *Jen*. He thought he had better apologize quickly. "I'm sorry. You told me to call you Jennifer. I didn't mean to take liberties with your name."

"It's quite alright. You can call me Jen. I haven't been called Jen in a long time."

Greg felt the weight of the manuscript and guessed it was around two hundred to two hundred fifty pages. "Are they going to perform the whole thing?"

"No. What I handed you is what I wrote. I just pulled parts from this for a simple play for the kids to perform."

"So, you're a writer and a teacher. You're very talented. Do you mind if I read it?"

"You're welcome to borrow the manuscript. I have other copies."

"Do you write a lot?"

"This makes my tenth book."

"Wow! Have any been published?"

"No. I wanted to be a novelist. I got an MFA in Creative Writing. I even had an agent who found a publisher for my first book."

"I thought you said you didn't have any books published," challenged Greg.

"Repeating your earlier statement, it's a long story."

A few people stood near the table, eyes fixated on Greg. Finally, one gathered enough courage to come forward to ask for an autograph, and he was then followed by the others. A few people asked if they could take selfies with Greg, and he agreed. As the waiter came to the table with their food, the autograph seekers retreated to their own tables, happily examining their evidence that they had indeed personally met the world wrestling champion.

"The food is here, buddy. Time to put up the phone."

Greg was about to take a bite when he noticed Jennifer looking at him.

"What?" asked Greg. "Have I already spilled food on myself?"

"No," smiled Jennifer. "I was just thinking. Do people always ask for autographs everywhere you go?"

"It's nothing like a famous actor would get out in public, but that could change if I get the movie role I auditioned for."

"You didn't tell me that you auditioned for a movie. Do you think you might get it?"

"My agent says it's between one other person and me. I have a good shot at landing it, and it would be good for my career. Look at how the Rock's, Dwayne Johnson's, movie career took off, and he was a wrestler."

"Well, if you get the part, I guess I'll have to stand in line to get your autograph."

"For you, I'd let you come to the front of the line."

Austin was already eating, and both Greg and Jennifer dug into their meals. Greg was pleasantly surprised at how good the food was. With all the Christmas decorations, he thought that maybe the restaurant used those, rather than good food, to entice people to come.

"Austin, you seem to be enjoying your meal," commented Jennifer.

"I'm hungry," replied Austin. "Dad made some green drink for me for breakfast that he called a power smoothie."

"He took one sip and spit it out," interjected Greg. "I don't think that green will ever come out of the carpet. I tried everything on it. Stephanie's going to kill me when she gets back."

Jennifer laughed, covering her mouth, which was full of food.

Austin continued. "I usually eat lunch at the school cafeteria, but dad made me a sandwich to take for lunch that was all soggy by lunch time. I didn't eat it. This is my first meal today."

"Oh no!" exclaimed Jennifer.

"Ok, son. You've embarrassed me enough for one night. Tomorrow you can eat in the cafeteria, and we'll pick something up on the way home for breakfast. What do you usually eat for breakfast?"

"Doughnuts!" answered Austin.

Greg and Jennifer looked at each other and laughed.

"I know your mother wouldn't let you eat that for breakfast. We'll find something between a green power smoothie and doughnuts that you'll eat and that will be healthy for you at the same time."

Walking on the sidewalk back to their cars after the meal at the restaurant, Greg was disappointed that the time spent with Jennifer that day was ending.

"Thank you for inviting me."

"Does this make us even for the diner episode?"

"Um ... close."

Kringle

The next couple of days, Greg developed a routine: take Austin to school, go to physical therapy, come home and do some housework and laundry, pick up Austin from school, cook simple dishes for dinner, do homework with Austin, and put him to bed. Greg wondered how Stephanie did this and work a full-time job as a Vice President. Still, Greg found comfort in the routine and discovered that he enjoyed spending time with Austin, even doing the mundane activities.

Thoughts of Jennifer inevitably forced their way into his mind, but he would push them aside. He wanted to see her. He wrestled with conflicting emotions, wanting to see her versus knowing that he didn't need to form an attachment that would end as soon as Stephanie returned.

As soon as Friday arrived, Austin was back to begging Greg about Christmas decorations. Greg was nervous about keeping Austin occupied for the weekend. On Saturday, he thought about trying to prepare something special for lunch and have leftovers that night. He knew he needed to improve his cooking, and he alternated between the two clichés of *dip your toe into the water* and *get back on the horse.* On one occasion he inadvertently combined the two in his thoughts to form *dip your horse into the water.* That one had at least caused him to chuckle.

Greg began early in preparing lunch, and it took an inordinate amount of time, he thought, to prepare it. Around eleven a.m., Austin came into the kitchen and sat on a stool, watching his dad cook. If cooking were like a wrestling match, it was winning. Realizing a little too late that cooking was not a linear process, he found himself juggling too many things at once. He thought that Austin probably found watching him more entertaining than playing on his phone at that point, but then Austin suddenly got up and rushed out of the room.

"Hey, dad! There's a dog barking at our door."

Greg walked into the room and found Austin looking out of the window towards the front door. He could hear the barking. It didn't sound like a big dog. Greg opened the door to walk outside, and Austin was right behind him. The dog sat as soon as Greg and Austin were outside. It was a medium-sized mixed breed dog that seemed very friendly. Greg tried to identify the parentage of the dog. It looked like a mix of beagle and Siberian retriever, but he was not an expert in identifying breeds.

Austin sat and began petting the dog. "Where did you come from, boy?"

Greg could see that the dog had a collar, and he was about to check the dog tag when he heard a voice call out.

"Kringle?"

"Over here," shouted Greg.

To Greg's surprise, Jennifer walked up holding a dog leash and a dog biscuit. He assumed the dog biscuit was to lure the dog, if necessary.

"There you are," cooed Jennifer in a voice one might use to talk to a baby. The dog stood up, wagged its tail, and trotted over to her. Jennifer looked up at Greg and began offering an explanation. "I opened the door, and Kringle just ran out. He never does that. I'm sorry if he bothered you."

"He probably smelled dad's cooking and came to warn us not to eat it!"

Greg raised one corner of his closed lips and exhaled sharply through his nose a sound that was a combination of laughter and embarrassment. "Very, funny, Austin. So ... Jen, even your dog has a Christmas name. You really are into Christmas."

Kringle barked. Jennifer knitted her brow and held her head in the air. She sniffed the air. Suddenly, she grew excited. "On no! I think something's burning."

Greg shouted, "The oven!" He turned and saw wisps of smoke coming through the open door and ran immediately into the kitchen with Austin and Jennifer running behind him. Bringing up the rear, was Kringle, who once again began barking.

Greg opened the door, which allowed even more clouds of smoke to pour out. He immediately used oven mitts to bring the dish out of the oven and set it on the stove while Jennifer opened some windows to let out the smoke. The smoke detector alarm went off, and Kringle barked even more. Fortunately, the smoke dissipated quickly, and the smoke detector ceased the alarm.

Greg, Jennifer, and Austin stood and stared at the burnt meal.

"Well, so much for that meal," announced Greg.

"I feel terrible," declared Jennifer. "If you hadn't been distracted by Kringle, you wouldn't have burnt … whatever that is. You and Austin can come over to my place. I prepared a big meal. My parents and sister are over. We'd love to have you join us."

"Thank you, but I don't want to intrude on family time."

"You won't be. They come over all the time. Besides, you can talk with my dad about wrestling. He coaches the high school team."

"Please, dad. Can we?"

"Alright," yielded Greg, "if you're sure it's not an inconvenience."

"Positive," affirmed Jennifer.

Ten minutes later, Greg and Austin were in Jennifer's house. Kringle trotted over to Austin and licked his hand. Austin immediately started playing with Kringle, who seemed excited to have the attention. "Don't run," admonished Greg. "Remember, this is not your house. We're guests."

"It's ok for them to play. Kringle loves kids. They won't cause any harm."

Greg hoped he had made the right decision. He did want to see Jennifer again and spend time with her, but being there with her family could also be awkward. Greg brought Jennifer's manuscript along to return it to her since he had finished reading it, but she wasn't near enough for him to give it to her. Greg smiled at the strangers who stood before him.

"Everyone, this is Greg Hunter and his son Austin," announced Jennifer. "Greg is watching Austin while Stephanie is away." Jennifer then introduced her family, pointing each one out to Greg and Austin. "This is my father, Harris Bell, my mother, Emily Bell, and my sister, Carol Bell. And you've met Kringle," she added, laughing.

"So, you're the dufus ... I mean the dad who is the professional wrestler," greeted Carol.

Greg wondered what Jennifer had told her sister. More than likely, it was the truth. "It's nice to meet everyone," smiled

Greg affably. "Thank you for allowing us to come over and join you."

"Greg Hunter, aka Hunter Savage," came the gruff voice of Coach Harris Bell. "I never thought you would go the professional wrestling route, but it's good to see you after all these years."

"What?" exclaimed Jennifer with a shocked expression on her face. "Have you met Greg before, dad?"

Coach Bell folded his arms and Greg felt as though he were being sized up as a high school student wanting to join the wrestling team. "Yes. I saw him several times when our team wrestled against his team. You were one of the best wrestlers I've ever seen, Greg."

"Thank you," replied Greg. "That means a lot." Greg's eyes suddenly grew wider. "Wait, I do remember you now."

Coach Bell smiled. "You know. I secretly pulled for you over some of my own team's wrestlers."

Jennifer seemed utterly flabbergasted. "Dad! Where's your school spirit?"

"You know him too, Jennifer."

"What? I never met him until recently."

"Don't you remember …" coach Bell was unable to complete the sentence. Carol noticed Greg holding something and jumped right into the conversation.

"What's that you're holding, Greg?' asked Carol.

By this point, Jennifer had moved closer to Greg. "I brought Jennifer her book back." He handed the manuscript to Jennifer. "I really enjoyed reading it. You are a great writer."

"Jennifer, did you write another book?" smiled Carol. "You really need to see about getting them published."

Greg hoped he hadn't started something or embarrassed Jennifer. She looked a little uneasy at Carol's question and comment.

"I enjoy teaching," replied Jennifer. "Besides, it has been too long to get back into that world. I threw away my shot at being an author."

Greg thought that Jennifer appeared a little downcast.

"You're just making excuses," retorted Carol.

Carol certainly seemed to be feisty, but Greg was glad she was taking it to Jennifer. The things Jennifer said were excuses, and she needed to know that it still wasn't too late.

The conversations that were going back and forth seemed to catch Austin's attention. He stopped playing with Kringle and trotted over. Something seemed to finally dawn on him, and he asked a question. "Is your name really Carol Bell?"

"I was born in December. Mom has this weird sense of humor. Believe me, I was kidded all through school. I used to dream about getting married just so I could change my last name, but I'd probably end up marrying someone with a last name like *Christmas*. Then when you have to say your last name first and first name last, I'd have to say *Christmas, Carol.*" The ease with which Carol answered made him think she had explained her name many times before.

"That would be cool," exclaimed Austin.

"Trust me. I don't want to find out," teased Carol as she stooped to Austin's eye level. "So, did your dad name you after a city where he was wrestling when you were born?"

"He did."

Carol hesitated, obviously embarrassed, thought Greg.

"At least he wasn't wrestling in North Pole, Alaska. Then you would be North Pole Hunter, and you would have a Christmas name better than mine."

"That would be really cool!" Austin's face lit up. "Did you ever wrestle in North Pole, Alaska, dad?"

"No. I don't believe so. I wrestled in Fairbanks. I think that's pretty close."

Carol was quick on her feet, thought Greg. He was a little embarrassed at what Jennifer's family may have thought about how Austin got his name. He was about to change the subject when Emily interjected.

"Carol, dear, I wish you would quit telling that story." Emily appeared exasperated as she shook her head in a way that made Greg think she had heard Carol explain her name hundreds of times before.

"It's retribution for naming me Carol. Jennifer is Ms. Christmas. You should have named her Carol."

"We have guests, you two. Enough with the ongoing name battle. Besides, Carol, you were the one born in December."

Emily quickly changed the subject. "Oh, Jennifer. I saw Steve yesterday at the market. Apparently, he's back in town. He asked about you."

From the look on Jennifer's face, Greg imagined that Jennifer wished she had let Emily and Carol continue their conversation. The mention of Steve, though, did make Greg a little curious, and a tinge of jealousy effused through him. "Who is Steve?" He tried to ask as nonchalantly and casually as possible, as if he were just trying to make conversation.

"Jennifer's only boyfriend," answered Coach Bell.

Greg looked to Jennifer, who appeared mortified at what her father had just said. Her face flushed almost immediately. She glanced at Greg and quickly turned her head away, angling it slightly toward the floor.

"Dad! You make me sound pitiful."

Greg was embarrassed for Jennifer. He wanted to tell her that he was basically in the same situation, although now was not the appropriate time to tell her. He met Stephanie in college and married her upon graduation. He had a few dates in high school, but wrestling, football, and training occupied much of his time. The majority of the times he went out were usually with groups of people. After his divorce, traveling from one city to another to wrestle allowed him practically no time to date.

Coach Bell seemed nonplussed at Jennifer's embarrassment and continued explaining who Steve was.

"They dated from the time she was sixteen until last Christmas when he broke up with her. He's the reason Jennifer gave up on a career as a writer." Coach Bell turned his gaze from Greg to Jennifer, and in a tone that Greg surmised was probably as close to begging as the coach's gruff exterior persona would allow added, "Please tell me you're not considering going back to that jerk."

Jennifer's face had now lost its earlier redness. Now she merely appeared perturbed. Her mouth was ajar and matched her widened eyes, which were creating small lines of tension etched above her eyebrows. "This is the first time I heard he was in town. The last I heard, he had a promotion that sent him to New York, and he was engaged to the CEO's daughter. You don't have to worry, dad. I'm not going through that again. I hardly ever saw him because he worked all the time. I want someone who puts family first."

"I'll find out what happened to bring him back to town," declared Emily in a determined-sounding voice.

"Mom! If you go asking around, he'll think I'm still interested." Jennifer's face had undergone yet another transformation to one that now had the appearance of annoyance.

"I'm not going to ask directly," countered Emily. "Give me some credit. I can offhandedly find out."

"There's nothing offhanded about your inquiries," chimed Carol.

Greg was only half paying attention to the conversation after Jennifer's declaration that Steve worked all the time, was never around, and that she wanted someone who put family first. In Greg's mind, that solidified his earlier reasoning of why he didn't need to become involved with Jennifer, even though he very much wanted to do so. Realizing where the current conversation might be headed, he decided to try to divert it before it went further down the road of Steve's situation and intention. "So, how is he the reason you're not a writer?"

Greg realized too late that this probably wasn't an easier avenue for Jennifer to go down. She looked like a rabbit caught between two foxes as her head turned one way, then the other. She must have resigned herself to the fact that she was going to have to relive the whole ordeal. "Steve thought writing was silly and that I shouldn't waste my time on writing. He said only a few people made a decent living with it and that I was better off teaching."

Before Jennifer could continue, Carol eagerly jumped in to finish the ending to Jennifer's and Steve's romance. "And when he broke up with her right at Christmas last year, he said she wasn't ambitious enough and that if he wanted to further his career, he needed someone besides an elementary school teacher."

Greg's mind winced just thinking about what he heard. That was a jerk move, he thought to himself.

"I don't want to talk about this anymore. Lunch is ready. Let's eat," commanded Jennifer.

Everyone shuffled around the dining room table, as if playing a game of musical chairs, until they found appropriate seats. Kringle circled around the table with them, and he was now wagging his tail and sniffing wildly at the aroma that had effused throughout the house. Kringle finally plopped down beside Austin. Greg suspected that Kringle knew who would either by accident or on purpose drop the most food.

Lunch was served, and the group ate quickly and silently for the most part. As people began to stir after eating, Coach Bell cleared his throat. "I have an announcement. I'm going to be retiring at the end of December."

Jennifer's and Carol's expressions of wide eyes and open mouths mirrored each other. Clearly, this was the first inkling that either had of their dad's decision.

Jennifer was the first to speak. "You're retiring in the middle of the year? Why?"

"I've coached and taught for forty years." Coach Bell's gruff voice sounded tired at just the mention of forty years of doing the same thing. "I'm ready to do something different."

"Have you given any thought to what you want to do?" asked Carol. "Surely, you're not planning on moving out of state, are you?"

Jennifer let out a gasp at the mention of their parents moving out of the state.

"Calm down," urged Coach Bell. "We're not planning on moving. And as for what I want to do, I'm not jumping into anything right away. I figure I'll give myself at least six months of relaxation and traveling and then see what comes to mind."

Greg noticed a weird eye and head motion that Coach Bell made at Emily, almost as if it were some signal the two shared between themselves.

"Besides," continued Coach Bell, "getting on the mat with high schoolers is tough on one's body. "

Emily chimed in, "Actually, your father hurt his back, and I don't think he should help you with your Christmas Tree today."

"Well, I ..." Carol had begun to say something but cut off quickly when Emily gave the same type of eye and head motion that her husband had given her. "I ... I ... can't help either. I ... uh ... got an unexpected assignment in my graduate course that I have to go home and work on."

Jennifer either had not seen the eye and head motions or didn't care. "You all do what you need to. I can put it up myself."

"Honey," began Emily in a very mom-sounding voice, "you don't want to hurt yourself putting up a tree by yourself. Maybe Greg wouldn't mind helping you."

"Christmas isn't really my …" Greg was cut off before he could finish the statement.

"Thank you for being such a gentleman, Greg," commended Coach Bell. "Now, if you'll excuse us, I need to go home and ice my back."

Emily stood immediately, and before Greg barely had time to blink, the two were through the door with Emily calling out for Carol.

"I'd better go too … to get started … on that … thing," explained Carol as she decamped from the house in the same style as her parents.

"Talk about eat and run," exclaimed Jennifer. "That was weird."

Greg turned to face Jennifer. His left eyebrow was raised while his right eyebrow scrunched closer to his eye. "Is this some scheme of yours to get me to do Christmas activities?"

A smirk formed on Jennifer's face that Greg wanted to reach in and kiss. "Yes. I told Kringle which house to go to. He carried out his part rather well, don't you think?"

"Can we help decorate Ms. Bell's tree dad? Please," pleaded Austin.

"The word you want to use is *may*," corrected Greg, "not *can*."

Austin continued looking at Greg, apparently oblivious to the grammar lesson.

"Alright," succumbed Greg. "Let's just get this over with. I'll go get it. Show me the garage."

"It's not in the garage," Jennifer remarked matter-of-factly.

"Ok. Where's your attic?"

Jennifer smiled, "It's not in the attic."

"Ok. Where is it?"

Jennifer was still smiling as she answered. "It's in the Christmas Tree lot down the street!"

"I thought you might have one of those trees that just unfolds with the lights already on them. It would be cheaper than buying a live tree every year. And better for the environment too."

"Part of the fun is picking out a tree and having that pine-tree smell in your house."

"They do sell pine-tree-scented air freshener," quipped Greg.

Within a few minutes everyone was dressed and ready to go to the Christmas Tree lot.

"Do you want me to drive?" asked Greg as he tidied the sleeve of his coat.

"It's just takes a couple of minutes to walk down the street?" replied Jennifer.

"Can we …" Austin stopped in midsentence when Greg squinted at him, and he correctly asked his question. "May we take Kringle with us?"

Jennifer looked over at Kringle, who was sleeping soundly after a few bites of food. "Let's leave him here. His belly is full, and he is probably dreaming about what he wants for Christmas this year."

The air felt great to Jennifer as they walked, brisk but not freezing. The town was decorated for Christmas; the lights were on. Several of the shops, though closed, were decorated and had their Christmas lights on. Jennifer hummed quietly as they wended down the street. Once they were in the Christmas Tree lot, she almost laughed as Greg turned serious, as if he were on an extraction mission to get in and out as quickly and as quietly as possible. An acting role in a movie about a Seal Team or Delta Force team would be a perfect fit for him, she thought.

"What kind of tree are you looking for?" Greg's head turned quickly in several directions looking for *the* tree.

"We'll know it when we see it."

"That's not very precise."

He's one of those people, thought Jennifer, the kind who wanted to know the exact height, circumference, and type of tree. She amusedly pictured him pulling out a tape measure. "Christmas is about feeling the Christmas Spirit. For the Christmas Tree for instance, you can't list a specific height or circumference or type of tree. You have to choose what speaks Christmas to you."

"I'm thinking about having to carry it back!"

"Don't worry. I'll help the muscular professional wrestler, who's used to picking up two hundred-and-fifty-pound men, carry it back. It's only a few blocks back to the house." Jennifer stopped, and Greg continued to walk with a purpose. "Stop."

"Do you see it?" asked Greg looking around.

"No. Come here."

Greg had a questioning look on his face as he shuffled back toward Jennifer.

Jennifer spread her arms out. "Do what I do."

"Ok." Greg paused. "Is this going to look silly?"

"Again, I'll help the professional wrestler, who's used to looking silly all the time on television."

"How do you know whether or not I look silly, if you've never seen me on tv?"

Jennifer ignored his quip. "Just do as I do."

Greg slowly held his arms out, parallel to the ground, to mimic Jennifer's. Austin scrutinized them curiously but came over and mimicked the stance. Soon all three were displaying the same stance.

"Now close your eyes, hold your head back with your nose pointed in the air, and take a deep breath through your nose." Jennifer laughed as she heard the exaggerated inhalation from Greg.

"Hey, no peeking," protested Greg.

"I don't have to peek to hear you sniffing like a bloodhound. Now, breathe deeply through your nose again but quieter this time." She waited a few seconds. "Tell me what you're sensing."

"I can smell green," gasped Austin.

"What do you sense?" asked Greg.

Jennifer deliberated for a few seconds. "I feel the cool night air on my face. I can smell the evergreen trees and the freshly cut wood. I hear the soft Christmas music playing in the background accompanied by the excited voices of people finding the trees that are perfect for them. I feel a peace that I wish I could rest in forever."

"Wow. You did a lot better than I did," exclaimed Austin.

"Not really. You smelled a color. I would say that's pretty good. Besides, there is no right or wrong answer. It all depends on how focused you are in paying attention to your senses.

Austin suddenly pointed to a large tree. "How about that one?"

"I think that's a little too big!"

"I think that's way too big!" Greg put his hand to his lower back as he spoke.

"What about that one?" Upon hearing that the tree was too big, Austin had already run to another tree.

Jennifer ambled over to inspect the latest prospect. "That one's got too many gaps in it."

"Glad you're not putting too many specific characteristics to it," proclaimed Greg facetiously. "You know, an artificial tree wouldn't have gaps."

Jennifer returned his comment with a facetious look of her own, and she said in a mildly annoyed tone, "Just keep looking."

"This one looks nice." Both Greg and Jennifer searched where Austin had just been standing, but he was gone.

"Where are you?" called Greg.

"Over here." Austin sounded as though he were in the middle of the lot.

Jennifer and Greg wound their way through the maze of evergreens, looking all around as they reached a new row. Finally, they saw him standing in front of a tree, pointing.

Once Jennifer had a good look at the tree to which Austin was pointing, she grew excited. "That's the one!" The tag indicated that the tree was a Fraser/Balsam Fir Hybrid. Greg flagged down a worker as she double checked to make sure that this was indeed the tree that spoke to her. It was of a good size but not too large. It was fairly symmetrical; the only trees that were completely symmetrical were artificial. She didn't see any prominent gaps in the limbs. The needles were firm and didn't come off in her hand as she pulled it along a few branches. The aroma was pleasantly piney. Yep. This was the one.

One of the workers hurried over; he appeared to be college aged. "I'll get it ready for you."

Jennifer was true to her word and helped Greg carry the tree back. She thought that he must have carried the majority of the tree's weight. Back at Jennifer's house, Greg pulled out a pocketknife to cut off the netting. He had almost made the mistake of cutting the netting before they had placed it in the tree stand. Jennifer had gone to get the tree stand and stopped him in the nick of time. "Amateur," she said playfully.

The worker had asked what kind of tree stand she had and had cut the bottom of the tree to the appropriate circumference. The tree fit nicely into the tree stand. Once it was secured and the netting had been cut away, Jennifer checked to make sure it wasn't leaning in one direction.

"Do you want to help decorate?" asked Jennifer.

"Yes!" replied Austin enthusiastically.

"We've done our part, Austin. Ms. Bell may want to decorate it herself."

He's not just being polite in suggesting to Austin that I may want to do it myself; he definitely doesn't want to decorate, thought Jennifer. I've got my work cut out for me if I'm to keep my promise to Stephanie.

Austin quickly jumped into the conversation. "But how's she going to reach the top of the tree? She might fall and hurt her knee like you did. Besides, mom wanted you to do Christmas things with me."

"Oh!" Jennifer instinctively put her hand to her mouth. "I forgot about your knee. I shouldn't have had you carry the Christmas Tree."

"Well, you did help me carry it. My knee is not that bad now, but I wouldn't want you to fall with no one here."

Greg volunteered to make hot chocolate while Jennifer laid out the decorations and planned the offensive of decorating. Austin assured her that his dad could at least make hot chocolate. When he came out with no marshmallows in the mugs of hot chocolate, Jennifer sent him back into the kitchen to retrieve marshmallows. Everyone sipped hot chocolate as Jennifer laid out the charge.

"Everyone needs to do as I ordered," declared Jennifer. "We don't need anyone going rogue."

"Yes, Sergeant," gibed Greg, which he quickly changed to, "Yes, Ms. Christmas," upon seeing her scowl. "Even though I'm not big into Christmas, I certainly admire your … er … enthusiasm regarding Christmas."

Jennifer crossed her arms and tapped her foot as she scowled at Greg. "What were you going to say in place of enthusiasm?"

Greg made a *beats me* gesture with bent elbows close to his body and palms facing up.

"Well, at least you've been forewarned about my … er … enthusiasm."

"Forewarned is forearmed as the saying goes."

In short order, they were putting the finishing touches on the tree. Jennifer's plan of attack had unfolded perfectly.

Jennifer plugged in the lights, and they all stood back to admire the tree and the work they had done.

"Hey, dad? May Ms. Bell help us decorate our tree?"

The look on Greg's face told Jennifer that he had not even thought about a tree for themselves.

"We're not going to decorate a tree. You've just decorated one. If your mom wants a tree, you can help her."

"But mom and I have always celebrated Christmas. First, we moved. Now, she's at training. Can't something be the same?"

"It's getting late buddy. We need to get home."

Once Greg and Austin left, Jennifer sat on the couch musing about the day she had. Kringle jumped up on the couch and snuggled against her, letting out a sigh that Jennifer interpreted as exhaustion. She thoroughly enjoyed the time she spent with Greg, and Austin too, that day. Greg was not the same person she had experienced the day he came to her room to talk about Austin or the person she encountered at the diner. Something about Greg made her feel giddy in a way that she had not felt before, even with Steve. Did Greg feel the same about her? She couldn't believe she was thinking about a relationship with someone she barely knew, but her feelings were at odds with her reasoning. As much as she liked Greg, any future relationship was out of the question. She had confessed as much at lunch. She didn't want another Steve, and work occupied as much of Greg's time as Steve's work had. However, as much as her head told her this couldn't work and to put Greg out of her mind, her heart would butt in and try to convince her otherwise.

Before she knew it, she had pulled up videos of Hunter Savage's wrestling matches along with some of his interviews. She found herself laughing hysterically at some of the interviews. Greg's alter ego of Hunter Savage certainly could put on quite the show. His flamboyant performance, his arrogance, the women who adorned him the way jewelry adorned rich women, all contributed to paint an image of a man that Greg seemed to be at their first meeting but was not at all the Greg she had seen afterwards. Was Hunter a part of Greg or merely a façade? Like Hunter, Greg was quick with quips, and he had an outgoing personality. But Hunter didn't have the tender heart that Greg constantly tried to hide. Greg was certainly an enigma, but he was an enigma that she was enjoying getting to know. She fast forwarded through or bypassed portions of the wrestling, but she gleaned enough to see the talent and showmanship Greg possessed.

Her dad saw Greg wrestle in high school; she wondered what he thought of the wrestling Greg did now. High school wrestling and professional wrestling were as different as night and day. The thought of her father watching professional wrestling had never even entered her mind, and she grew tickled at the thought of him watching it and throwing punches at an imaginary adversary. That definitely was not her dad's style. She could see her mother doing that but not her dad!

When Jennifer spied the clock, she was shocked to see how much time she had spent watching videos online. She enjoyed it, but she would pay the price for it tomorrow when she needed to get out of bed.

Practice and Promise

On Monday, when Greg picked Austin up at school, he could tell something was bothering him. Austin remained quiet on the ride home. Once he sailed into the house, he dropped his bookbag on the floor.

"What's wrong, buddy? You've been quiet since I picked you up from school."

Austin hung his head and stared at the floor as he spoke. "We're having tryouts this week for the candy cane relay at school. I can't do it, and nobody wants me on their team."

Before Greg could say anything, Austin was running upstairs to his room. Greg went to the kitchen to begin preparing dinner, but Austin's disappointment haunted his thoughts. And of course, his disappointment had to center around a Christmas activity. If karma could be personified as a wrestling opponent, Greg would certainly lose every bout. What was it about Christmas that would not leave him be?

Austin's depressed mood continued through dinner that night. Greg had finished eating what he thought was actually a decent meal, but Austin was lost in thought, playing with his food.

"Grab your coat, Austin. We're going out."

Austin looked up, surprise showing on his face. "Where are we going?"

"It's a surprise." Greg was torn between a smile and a frown, and he came off sounding as gruff as Coach Bell.

Greg and Austin climbed into Stephanie's Ford Escape, and Greg drove a few houses down before pulling into Jennifer's driveway.

Austin seemed surprised, but he didn't say anything. Inside Jennifer's house, Kringle jumped up and down excitedly around Austin as though he were doing some ritual dance. Curiosity must have finally gotten the better of Austin, and he asked, "What are we going to do here?"

"We're going to help train you for the candy cane relay tryouts," replied Greg. "I figured if anyone had candy canes, it would be Ms. Bell, and she would also know the format of the relay."

Greg assumed that the candy cane relay involved hooking candy canes together and transferring them to the next person in the relay team, but that was not the version for this relay at all. This version of the relay required one to balance a candy cane on one's finger while walking a certain distance before transferring it to the next person.

Greg and Jennifer worked with Austin on balancing a candy cane on his finger. It was slow going. Austin dropped and broke a good many candy canes in what seemed like thirty minutes of practice. Greg wondered if even Jennifer had enough candy canes for the practice. Eventually, Austin was able to balance the candy cane. Now they had to conquer transporting it the required distance. It took quite a while, but Austin was finally able to walk across the room while balancing it, even while Greg, Jennifer, and Kringle tried to distract him. Austin was able to make several successful trips without dropping it. Now came the hard part. Transferring it to another person without dropping it and without causing the other person to drop it. After several tries, Austin seemed to get the knack for it, and Austin's earlier moodiness had completely passed.

"Way to go, buddy," encouraged Greg. Austin took a break to play with Kringle, and Greg took Jennifer to the side to talk with her. "Thanks for your help. I have another huge favor to ask you."

"Sure," replied Jennier, who seemed to have had as much fun as Austin had when he finally got the knack of the game.

"The GWO is going to be in Louisville, Kentucky tomorrow night, and they want me to promote my match at *Winter Frenzy*. It will be early in the segment, and I can leave afterwards, but I would get home late. Most of my time will be driving there and back, and Austin would have to be by himself when I'm doing my segment."

"Are you asking so that you get to drive your Porsche there and back or for legitimate concern for Austin." Jennifer was smiling as she said it and Greg hoped that was her way of teasing him, but he wasn't one hundred percent sure. "I'm teasing," she finally admitted. "He can stay with me."

"It will be late by the time I can get back to pick him up. Are you sure you don't mind?"

"It's no problem, but you must promise that you'll do something for me in return."

"Isn't quid pro quo some violation of teacher ethics?" Greg teased.

"Do you promise or not?"

"I promise. Anything. Just name it."

"I'll tell you after you get back!"

The Full House

Greg did drive the Porsche to Louisville and back, changing to Stephanies Ford Escape between dropping Austin off and picking him up. When Greg arrived at Jennifer's house, the hour was late, and Austin was asleep on the couch with Kringle lying at his feet.

"Thanks so much for doing this. You're a lifesaver." A scent wafted to Greg's nose, and he sniffed the air. "What is that smell? It smells like a bakery in here."

Jennifer replied coyly, "Austin said you wouldn't make Christmas Cookies with him; so, we made some tonight. I hope you don't mind."

"No. that's fine. You didn't have to go to all that trouble though."

"It was no trouble," insisted Jennifer. She strayed toward the kitchen and Greg unconsciously followed her.

"Do you want to try one of the cookies?"

Greg didn't, but he also did not want to hurt Jennifer's feelings; so, he quickly came up with an excuse that sounded legitimate. "Thanks, but … I need to stay away from sugar while my knee is recuperating. My physical therapist says that sugar is not good for joints or ligaments or something another when trying to recuperate."

Jennifer seemed to buy the rationale. "Of course, we had to watch your part on tv tonight. You really turn it on in front of the camera."

"That's what I do. I can't believe you actually watched!"

"I also watched some videos online last night of you wrestling," she confessed.

"Really?" Greg was surprised at this revelation, but he also found comfort that Jennifer had taken the time to watch some of his matches.

"Well, the kids talk about wrestling all the time. I had to see what the fuss was all about."

Greg secretly hoped that was not the real reason that Jennifer had watched the videos. He hoped, that in part, the reason she watched was that she was beginning to feel for him the way he felt about her. He found the courage to ask, "What did you think?"

"Do you always end the match with the same move? Did I use the right terminology?"

The question pleasantly surprised him.

"It's called a *finisher*. It's a wrestler's signature move."

"That seems like it would be predictable to an opponent. Why not change it up?"

Greg appreciated the thoughtful analysis she provided on what she did know from the little she had seen of professional wrestling. "Well, that would be logical, but fans expect to see the same finisher. It's all part of the show, and each wrestler has a name for their finisher."

"What is your finisher called?" She leaned in closer. A few weeks ago, she would have been bored by a conversation about professional wrestling. Now, she eagerly took in every word.

"Well, it has to do with cards. It goes along with my catchphrase of the best player in the game and my merchandise, especially T-shirts showing playing cards."

"Let me guess. Royal Flush," teased Jennifer.

"Funny but no."

"The Ace Buster."

"Another funny one. I should have known you before I came up with the name."

"Ok. I give up. Tell me."

"Give up." Greg repeated two of the words she had just said. "Is that your idea of a wrestling pun?"

"Yeah. Pretty bad, wasn't it."

"Yeah," laughed Greg. "My finisher is called the Full House."

Jennifer could feel a look of perplexity appear on her face. "But a full house can be beaten by four of a kind."

"I didn't say it was the greatest name."

"Yep," teased Jennifer. "You should have let me name it."

Greg smiled, and a slight head movement must have allowed his eyes to catch sight of something. He looked up, and Jennifer's eyes followed. They were standing underneath mistletoe over the doorway leading into the kitchen. Jennifer hadn't noticed that they stopped directly underneath it. She had forgotten she had even put it there. As their heads lowered from looking up at the mistletoe, their eyes met. Jennifer gazed into blue eyes the color of the church domes on the Greek isle of Santorini. She finally understood the expression, *eyes that you could dive into and swim in*. That's exactly what she wanted to do. She felt as though their eyes were drawing them closer, begging for their lips to touch.

"It's late. I need to let you get to bed, and I need to get Austin home."

The surreality of the moment ended abruptly. It was as though Jennifer's soul was suddenly sucked back into her body, and she was once again in the present moment. Greg had started to lean in towards her, but then he suddenly ended it. She wanted to say something, but words wouldn't come to her.

"By the way," continued Greg, "what's this favor I owe you?"

Jennifer smiled mischievously. "You and Austin come to the town's Christmas event this Saturday."

Greg looked irritated, the way she imagined she looked when explaining something for the umpteenth time. "I don't do … "

"Yes. I know," Jennifer butted in before he could continue. "You don't do Christmas, but you did make a promise in exchange for Austin staying here. Plus, I'm taking advantage of the situation to try to win the challenge we made with each other."

Greg made a huffing noise that Jennifer took as a mixture of amusement and submission. "That's hitting below the belt!" He scratched the back of his head and hesitantly uttered, "But I won't break a promise."

Jennifer had a difficult time falling asleep that night. The thought of the *almost kiss* kept going through her mind, that and Greg's scintillating smile and Greg's deep blue eyes and … well, she could go on and on. It was a combination that made her weak-kneed. In fact, she had actually stumbled in place while standing under the mistletoe. All of the excitement now prevented her from sleeping, and she tossed and turned in bed.

Probably, two hours passed before she finally drifted off to a dream-filled sleep of Christmas activities with Greg and Austin.

The rest of the week passed slowly for Jennifer. Not a day had passed that she hadn't thought about Greg. Greg came by the next three afternoons during rehearsal for the play, but Jennifer was busy directing and couldn't talk with him. They talked briefly after the rehearsals on two occasions, but the conversations were casual. On the third afternoon, Helen sashayed into the auditorium, which she never did for rehearsals. Jennifer stole glances whenever she could. Every time, Helen always seemed to be giggling, and Greg was smiling. Helen rushed off shortly before the rehearsal ended, and Jennifer talked with Greg for about ten minutes.

Greg called on Friday night to make sure they were still going to the town's Christmas Fair on Saturday, and they talked for over an hour on the phone. Greg seemed interested in her, and she was definitely interested in him. She hoped she wasn't misreading the signals.

Wrestling with a Christmas Tree

Saturday morning, Greg and Austin walked the short distance to Jennifer's house. She had volunteered to drive; Greg was certain it was for the sole purpose of preventing him from leaving the Christmas event early. Although he wasn't looking forward to an event-filled day of Christmas-themed activities, he was definitely looking forward to spending time with Jennifer. If the price he had to pay to spend a day with her was to go to this town's Christmas thing, it was well worth it.

Greg suspected that Jennifer was the type of person who would leave ahead of time in order to arrive on time, if not early. Although that wasn't him, he purposely planned to arrive at Jennifer's house five minutes before she said they would leave. The event opened at 9:00 a.m., and it would take about twenty minutes or more to drive, park, and get to the gate; so, Jennifer suggested they leave at 8:30 a.m. He looked at his watch and noticed that it was 8:25 a.m. on the dot when he rang Jennifer's doorbell. Kringle began barking at the noise and was still barking when Jennifer opened the door.

"You're early!" she exclaimed with a surprised look on her face. "I didn't think you would show up until around 8:45!"

"I figured you for the early type; so, I tried to make sure I was early."

"Am I that easy to read that you know me so well already? Women are supposed to be mysterious and difficult to read."

"I just figured you for the early type. I make no claims in terms of being able to read you beyond that," chuckled Greg. "Well, let's go, if you're ready."

"What about Kringle?" asked Austin. "Is he going to be able to stay inside all day and not have to go to the bathroom?"

"That's very nice of you to be so concerned about Kringle. My next-door neighbor is going to let him out."

Jennifer grabbed her coat and the three of them got into Jennifer's car to head to the festivities. The drive only took fifteen minutes, and although they had arrived early, several cars had arrived before them. Jennifer parked in a paved lot, and they all got out and walked. Greg wondered where all the cars would park as more people came in.

They made their way to the entrance where a greeter took the admission fee and greeted people as they entered. He looked to be in his sixties, and he was dressed in a mishmash of Christmas garb. An arch covered with an assortment of Christmas wreaths stood over the greeter, and a row of decorated live trees extended from each end of the arch lining the entrance path. Even before entering, Greg could smell the greenery mixing in with other scents, such as apple cider, cinnamon, and ginger.

When it was their turn to enter, Greg paid the admission fee and was about to enter when the greeter stopped him. "Everybody has to pick a funny Christmas name. Pick one slip of paper from each Frosty the Snowman Hat," requested the greeter. "And make sure you keep them in the right order."

Jennifer plucked pieces of paper from each hat, and Greg and Austin followed suit. Once they had each picked their slips of paper, they moved along to make way for others to enter.

Austin couldn't keep still. "What's your name, dad?"

He studied the two pieces of paper, one in each hand, before answering, "Ebenezer Grinchface."

Jennifer and Austin simultaneously burst out in laughter.

"Let me see. That can't be right," declared Jennifer. "They don't usually have names like that. I've never seen one like that, ever."

"Oh, it is," retorted Greg, "and it's not funny. What is yours, Ms. I already have a last name that's Christmassy?"

Jennifer laughed as she read out her Christmas name. "Tickle Me McJingletoes."

"How do you have three names?" probed Greg.

"*Tickle me* is on the first slip of paper."

Then, Austin chimed in. "Mine is Sparky Gigglepants."

"That sounds about right!" commented Greg.

The three toured the downtown area admiring all the Christmas decorations. Greg was surprised at how many decorations the town had. They weren't tacky though. Much care and thought had been put into meticulously decorating this Christmas wonderland. He thought about all the work that had been done and was impressed that people did this every year, probably in addition to decorating their houses. "I'm surprised you don't have this many Christmas decorations," goaded Greg.

"If I had your salary rather than my teacher's salary, I might!"

Greg jolted his arm out suddenly, stopping Jennifer and Austin. "Whoa." Ahead was a person dressed as Santa Claus standing beside a donation bucket. He was joyfully ringing a bell as people put donations into the bucket. "Why do they let people do that? You can't go anywhere this time of year without people wanting money. Let's go this way to avoid solicitor Santa." Greg pointed to an alleyway to their left.

"What? No way. We're giving, Mr. Ebenezer Grinchface."

"What's a solicitor?" asked Austin.

"That's one of Santa's Reindeer." Greg was rather pleased with himself at his quick response to Austin's question. Jennifer's laugh pleased him even further. Greg put some money into the bucket, and Santa thanked him, handing out three miniature candy canes, one to each of them. "I think Santa is coming out way ahead. He's receiving a lot more in donations than these mini candy canes cost."

"You're not supposed to give in order to receive something back. You give from the abundance of your heart. The Christmas name you received really does suit you."

Greg knew she was right, but he wasn't used to this type of giving. In his experience, giving was always transactional. You gave so that you could get something back at some point, and you always reminded the person that it was now their turn to give as part of the transaction.

They hadn't gone too far past Santa when they came to a crowd gathered around something. Greg looked closer and saw that the crowd was gathered around a piñata. It was a Grinch piñata. Children were begging for someone to bust it open.

"This is right up your alley, Ebenezer Grinchface."

Greg appreciated the irony of Jennifer's comment.

"Try it, dad."

The look on Austin's face told Greg that he couldn't say no. He swaggered up, and the crowd parted to let his muscular frame pass through.

"Whoa," exclaimed the attendant. "Here's someone who can show this Grinch a thing or two." The attendant reached up with his arms fully extended as he blindfolded Greg. He awkwardly tried to spin Greg around, and Greg helped by spinning himself around several times. The attendant handed

Greg the stick. "Everybody, get out of his way. You don't want this guy hitting you instead of the piñata!"

Greg had no idea where the piñata was in relation to him, but he swung hard. He heard a thud and loud cheers from the crowd. The attendant took off the blindfold, and Greg watched the crowd of children eagerly picking up the spilled contents. Austin was among the crowd of children as well, picking up candy.

Austin came running back with two handfuls of candy. "Wow, dad. That was awesome. You got it on the first try."

"What can I say. I'm the Best Player in the Game."

The smirk on Jennifer's face was the cutest thing he had ever seen.

Austin and Jennifer both laughed at hearing Greg's famous tagline. Austin stuffed the candy into his pockets, keeping one out to eat as they passed more Christmas decorations. Soon, they came up to a big hill where people were sliding down on the packed snow.

"What's that?" asked Austin.

"That's a sled bowling game," answered Jennifer. "Remember, I said that this town really has some unique Christmas games and activities."

"Oh, I see now. Let's try that." Austin was excitedly jumping up and down. "It looks like lots of fun. You slide down the hill on a sled and try to knock over all the plastic Santa Clauses."

"I've never wrestled Santa Claus before, although I did wrestle someone dressed as a clown once. I'm game. Let's give it a try."

Austin ran over and picked out a large sled. Greg carried it over to a vacant lane and held the sled in place as Austin climbed in front.

Greg looked over and saw Jennifer standing nearby and smiling. Although she wore mittens, she rubbed her hands together to keep them warm. "Oh no. You're not getting out of this. Climb in here behind Austin in front of me."

Jennifer obliged and sat down behind Austin. Greg pushed the sled to the edge of the hill and got on just as it began its descent. He heard the thrill in Austin's scream and felt the cold wind hit his face. Jennifer leaned back against him laughing. They picked up speed as the sled barreled down the hill toward the targets. The sled ploughed into the plastic Santa Clauses, scattering them in various directions. As the sled came to a stop, Austin tumbled off the sled and rolled into the snowbank at the bottom of the hill.

Austin leapt up, covered in snow and laughing. "That was fun." He looked around at the knocked down Santas. "We knocked them all down in one try." An attendant ran out to reset the downed Santas.

Greg rolled off on the right side of the sled, protecting his knee. The crunching sound the snow made reminded him of the crunching sound his knee had made when he injured it. He helped Jennifer up, and they all stood there exhilarated by the ride. Jennifer was watching Austin brush the snow off himself, and Greg watched Jennifer. Strands of brownish auburn hair protruded from underneath the knit cap she wore and surfed the breeze, holding onto a breeze like a wave before falling down only to be picked up by the next wave-like breeze. Jennifer turned to him, her face beaming with a wide smile. The smile slowly faded when she noticed Greg looking at her, and her face showed the same desire as Greg thought his face must be showing. They stared at each other for a brief moment, sharing the desire between them before Austin ran up hugging them both. Greg felt drained, as if the desire had burned all the fuel within him.

"What's next?" inquired Austin.

"Slow down, buddy. We're here all day. Hey, what happened to your finger?" Greg noticed a small amount of blood coming from an apparent scratch.

"I don't know," replied Austin. "I didn't feel anything."

Jennifer swooped in. "It's just a minor scratch. I'll take care of it." She pulled some hand sanitizer out of her large purse and sprayed the cut. Austin winced a little from the sting of the alcohol in the hand sanitizer. Next, Jennifer pulled an adhesive bandage from her purse and put it on the cut on Austin's finger.

"What all do you have in your purse?" asked Greg. He wondered how much her purse weighed.

"A variety of things. As a teacher, one must be prepared for all sorts of emergencies."

Greg noticed that the bandage on Austin's finger was Christmas themed. "You really are Ms. Christmas, aren't you? Even the bandages you brought are decorated for Christmas."

"Tis the season after all," smiled Jennifer.

"Now, what's next?" asked Austin, a little irritated.

Austin can't sit still for long, thought Greg.

"I have an idea," interjected Jennifer. "Follow me." She marched determinedly up the hill with Austin at her heels and Greg a little behind.

"Slow down," called Greg. "I forgot that we had to walk back up the hill."

"You heard Austin. We only have one day. We have to get in as much as we can." Jennifer turned around. "Oh, is your knee bothering you?"

"No, but I don't want to go too fast and risk it acting up. I haven't done any physical therapy in a couple of days."

"I'm sorry. Let's slow down, Austin."

Austin obeyed, but Greg thought he did so begrudgingly. Once they made it to the top of the hill, Jennifer put her arm underneath Greg's for support. Greg relished her touch and wasn't about to tell her that really wasn't going to help if his knee had been hurting.

"Do you want to sit down?" she asked as they approached a bench.

"No. I'm fine. Really." He noticed how antsy Austin was; he couldn't keep still. "Where's this next activity you're taking us to?"

"Right over there."

Greg followed her finger and noted a big sign that read, *Paint your Own*. Underneath the sign were several doors.

As they strolled toward their next destination, Jennifer explained the activity. "They have thick papers of different colors. You pick the color you want, and the attendants hang them over the doors. They have cutouts for the doorknob. There are lots of condiment bottles filled with different colors of paint, containers of paint with brushes, and containers with glitter."

Austin was excited. "Let's do this. We can hang it on our door at home." Austin began opening the doors and running in and out. Greg stopped him at seeing the look on the attendant's face.

"I don't know. It looks pretty messy."

"Aw. Come on, dad. Where's your Christmas spirit?

"Yeah. Where's your Christmas spirit?" goaded Jennifer.

"I think I gave it to Santa when I gave that huge donation," joked Greg.

Jennifer jovially gave Greg a friendly shove.

"Ok. Ok. I know when I'm outnumbered. We'll do it."

"Yeah." Austin jumped up and down. "Let's work together, dad."

"Fine by me. I can use all the help I can get. Art never was a talent of mine."

For the next half hour, Greg and Austin worked on their door decoration with Austin haphazardly squirting multiple colors of paint and throwing glitter. When Austin had finally had enough of the artistic endeavor, they stood back to take in the masterpiece they had created.

"What do you think, buddy?"

"I think it's pretty ugly."

Greg laughed. "Well, it seems you took after me when it comes to art." Greg motioned for the attendant to come over and take down their paper. The attendant showed no emotion over the artwork. Either he was just doing his job or he had seen his share of ugly door decorations. "We have to let them dry. We can pick them up on the way out."

"It may be ugly, but it sure was fun."

They made their way over to Jennifer, who was putting the final touches on her door hanging.

"Wow, Jen. Yours looks great."

"It's all of those years decorating bulletin boards."

"Are you ready for lunch?" inquired Jennifer.

"Sure. I'm starving," replied Greg. "What do you want to eat?"

Jennifer reached into her purse. "I did take the liberty of bringing something." She pulled out three sandwiches. "They're turkey sandwiches. I didn't bring anything to drink though."

Greg had a look of shock on his face. "Are you sure there are no drinks in there? You must have a bottomless purse. How do you ever find anything?"

"It's certainly not easy sometimes."

"There is a drink stand over here," pointed Greg. A memory sprang into Greg's mind of his mother. He had to have been younger than Austin, but the memory was as clear as if it had happened yesterday. It was after Thanksgiving, and his mother had made turkey sandwiches with the leftover turkey. He remembered her serving his dad, himself, and herself each a cold glass-bottled Coca-Cola to go with the turkey sandwiches. She said it had always been a tradition in her house. It was a simple meal, but it was delicious. Greg couldn't help but grow melancholy at the thought. They found a small outdoor table next to the drink stand, and Greg bought a Coke for each of them for old times' sake.

As they were finishing eating, Greg noticed puffy, chocolatey clouds in the shape of scoops of ice cream begin to dot the sky. Soon the puffy clouds began to release small flakes of snow that floated and were jostled by the air like dust particles. Shortly, the flakes grew bigger. One gently kissed Jennifer's nose before evaporating against her skin. As silly as it was, Greg envied the snowflake. After a few minutes the snow stopped, but the snow was probably not finished for the day by the looks of the clouds.

"Hey, look over there!" Austin grabbed Greg's arm and pulled in the direction he was looking. "It's a wreath toss game where you try to throw the wreath over the head of a yard-ornamental reindeer."

Where does all of this energy come from, thought Greg. Maybe he'll eventually wear himself out. "Go for it, buddy."

"Dad! It's Sparky Gigglepants, not Buddy!" Greg and Jennifer were still rooted in place. "Aren't you and Ms. Bell coming?"

"I think we'll sit this one out. Sorry, Sparky. Stay where I can see you."

Jennifer got up and said she was going to take advantage of the time to look at some of the Christmas stands in the Christmas Market section, which was right beside of the table. She has as much energy as Austin, thought Greg.

Greg called out to Austin who was already running to the ring toss game. "There's a Christmas stand over here that Ms. Bell has already wandered off to. Stay where I can see you."

Austin turned around. "You already told me that."

"That means it's important that you listen."

Greg walked over to Jennifer, who was standing at a Christmas stand with jewelry. Greg glanced quickly to the ring toss game to see Austin toss a wreath at the head of a plastic reindeer. Jennifer's attention was engrossed in the jewelry. He liked it when all three of them did things together, but he was also glad to spend some time alone with Jennifer. "See anything you like?"

"What … Oh, sorry. I'm a sucker for jewelry."

"I can see that. You were drawn here like a ferromagnetic material to a magnet."

"That's mighty big word you used there."

"For a wrestler?"

"I wasn't thinking that. You've shown yourself to be very smart. Don't say it again."

"Yes ma'am."

Jennifer laughed. "Have you bought any Christmas presents yet?"

"No. I haven't been to the grocery store yet."

Jennifer's head jerked back slightly, and she furrowed her brows. "What are you giving people, a canned ham?"

"That's where the most gift cards are."

Jennifer made a muffled snorting noise. "Surely you don't just give all gift cards."

"I don't really have anyone to buy for, except Austin." That sounded sad when he heard himself say the words.

"Is that what you give Austin?"

Greg smiled, "A canned ham?"

Jennifer rolled her eyes in a playful and attractive manner. "No, gift card."

"Yes. It's a practical gift. You don't have to worry about exchanges or if the person likes it or not. Plus, they're easy to mail. This year, I thought about giving him wrestling figures, including one of me, and a wrestling ring to go with them."

"Is that what Austin really wants?"

Greg wondered what was wrong with that. He thought it was a pretty good gift idea. "Austin watches wrestling."

"He watches it to see his dad, but does he really like wrestling? He might would rather have something else." Jennifer paused. "Do you help Austin shop for his mom?"

"I haven't." Greg looked into the air in rumination. "I haven't really thought about it. I guess I should. Wow, how insensitive of me."

"Don't beat yourself up over it. Just do something about it."

Austin finished the game and ran over to his dad.

"Did you win anything, Sparky?"

"Nah."

"Hey, do you mind if I go over to a few more booths?" asked Jennifer.

"Not at all. Austin and I will be around here. We may sit and rest a while." At least Greg hoped they would sit and rest awhile. Austin seemed to want to remain constantly on the go.

Jennifer left and glided along the row of stands. Austin looked at the jewelry on the table. He pointed to a necklace. "Do you think mom would like this for Christmas?"

"If you pick it out, I'm sure she will love it."

"I think mom would like it."

It was a nice choice, and Greg thought she would like it too. "I'll buy it for you to give her, and we can wrap it later."

A few tables over, Jennifer looked up to see Greg paying the vendor for a necklace. He held it up, seemingly admiring it. It was a beautiful necklace. He shut the case and put the necklace case into his pocket. She turned back around and continued looking at the various stands.

Greg and Austin sauntered to a nearby bench and sat while they waited for Jennifer. Greg was glad to sit for a while. After about twenty minutes, Jennifer came back with a bag.

"They have the nicest things here. I bought several presents."

"I can tell. Since you also have your purse, let me help you carry some of the shopping bags."

"Did you find anything?

"I'm not much of a shopper." He wasn't sure why he didn't tell her he bought a necklace for Austin to give Stephanie. He supposed because it was really Austin's present to give, Austin should be the one to decide who should know. He had only paid for the present.

"Well, I found something for you." Jennifer handed him a large coin about two inches in diameter.

Greg received the coin with a puzzled expression on his face. "Is this to give to the next Santa Claus who asks for donations?"

"No. You need to use real money for that. I thought we already had this conversation. I bought it because you always seem to have lots of energy. That is, when you're not sitting on a bench about to fall asleep. It's a Christmas fidget coin. I know it's not much, but you'll have something to fidget with, if you ever need to release some nervous energy."

Greg accepted the coin and turned it between his fingers. He often did have nervous energy. He supposed that Austin inherited that from him because Austin seemed to have that same nervous energy, which he was definitely demonstrating today. "You know me well. Thank you. I'll keep this with me wherever I go."

Snow began falling again, harder than it had earlier and with much bigger flakes. The ground was cold, allowing the snow to stick. They strolled along a different part of town looking at more Christmas decorations and went into several shops. The stores were generally more expensive than the stands at the Christmas Market; so, they mostly just looked. After about an hour of shopping, Austin was getting bored; so, Greg let him play a few more Christmas-themed games. The snow had stopped, but about two inches of snow was on the ground. Even Greg had to admit to himself that the day embodied the holiday spirit.

"Oh, we can make it to the Christmas tree lighting if we head that way now," stated Jennifer.

"Let's go." Greg stood up from the bench.

"Is it that late already? Today just flew," moaned Austin.

Greg, Jennifer, and Austin arrived about twenty minutes before the tree lighting was to begin. A lot of people had already gathered around, but they still found a good spot to watch the tree lighting. Eventually, a man whom Jennifer identified as the mayor came out. He appeared to be in his fifties. He was dressed as a Victorian-period Christmas Caroler. Gray hair jutted out from underneath the tall Victorian hat. The mayor had large gray sideburns that went about halfway down his face. Greg thought that they looked real and were not the fake kind that some of the other carolers wore.

Greg turned in time to see a man approaching him. "Greg Hunter? Do you remember me?"

"I can't say that I do." Greg searched his memory, but no prior meetings came to mind.

"Greg, this is Steve Ross."

"Your ex-boyfriend," replied Greg. So, Steve wasn't approaching him; he was coming to see Jennifer.

Steve almost whispered to Jennifer, "Can we walk over to the side? I want to talk with you."

As Jennifer and Steve escaped the crowd, jealousy surged through Greg's veins like a rush of caffeine. He felt betrayed; he didn't know why. He had not known Jennifer that long. Why and how had he already developed such strong feelings for her? Perhaps it was puppy love or infatuation. He had not felt this way about Stephanie, and Stephanie was a very attractive woman too. Of course, Stephanie and he began as friends and never seemed to evolve from there. He didn't like feeling this way now. Perhaps he needed to go cold turkey and just stop seeing Jennifer, but the thought was heartbreaking.

Jennifer and Steve walked about twenty feet away from the crowd near the tree.

"You're not dating him, are you?" challenged Steve.

Jennifer ignored the question. "What do you want, Steve?" Jennifer had replied in a callous, uncompromising tone. Her insides were tied in tight knots, yet she displayed a deceptively unruffled exterior.

Steve calmed. "I hoped I would see you here, knowing how much you like Christmas and how we used to come to this every year. Did your mother tell you we talked?"

"She did," replied Jennifer with a voice and facial expression that was as unstirred as a placid pond.

Jennifer detected a look of regret on his face. "I made a big mistake," he began in a soft, broken voice. "I'm sorry I hurt you. It was my fault completely. I really missed you this past year. I was hoping maybe we could see each other some and try to rekindle what we had."

Although Steve said the right words, which seemed heartfelt, Jennifer could not easily forget the pain and betrayal he had put her through. Even if she correctly discerned his contrition, what he was asking was almost a bridge too far for her to cross. Images of Steve's breakup with her flooded her mind, reminding her that she could not be too cautious in believing him. Even if she forgave him, forgetting was a lot to ask of her. She became acutely aware that Steve was awaiting a response and that she had become lost in her own thoughts.

"Is that because your fiancée broke up with you, and since her father was the CEO of the company, he let you go?" Although she had tried to provide a response void of sarcasm, she had not been successful in delivering it.

Steve's head jerked back slightly as though he was taken aback by her response. His glistening face seemed out of place with the cold air that the night had brought in. "No," he stammered. "I just wasn't myself after we broke up, and I couldn't get over you."

Steve's words didn't jibe with her recollection of their breakup. He broke up with her because of the CEO's daughter. It wasn't a consequence of the breakup. Still, she had dated him for almost fifteen years, and that was a lot of time to just throw away.

Jennifer's conflicting thoughts were interrupted by the mayor's announcement. "It's almost time to light the Christmas Tree."

"It's time for the tree lighting. I really want to see this."

As she turned to leave, Steve gently grabbed her arm. "Just think about what I said. That's all I'm asking." Then he let go, and Jennifer made her way back into the crowd.

The mayor held up his arms and pushed down a few times to indicate to the crowd to get quiet. Once the talking died down, the mayor spoke. "We are going to pick someone to light the Christmas tree." Before he could say anymore, another man dressed as a caroler approached the mayor and whispered into his ear. The mayor raised his eyebrows questioningly but then began nodding his head as the other caroler continued whispering. Finally, the caroler stopped whispering and stood back. Conversation in the crowd had picked up again, and the mayor repeated the hand gesturing that he had made earlier to get the crowd to quiet down. "I hear we have World Wrestling Champion Hunter Savage in the crowd. Hunter Savage, would you come up and do the honors?"

The crowd chanted "Hunter" several times.

"Here. Hold this for me. Greg handed the fidget coin to Jennifer, who had a blank expression on her face. Greg made his way through the crowd smiling, high fiving, and fist bumping people as he went along.

Upon hearing the mayor's announcement and the words *Hunter Savage*, a fire of jealousy and spite descended on Steve like a mountain blizzard. Steve made his way behind some food and beverage stands. He passed only a few vendors, who gave questioning looks. The food and beverage stands provided perfect cover and all but abutted the towering Norway Spruce. He weaved his way undetected until he was in a position behind the tree. Steve was in the perfect location to be undetected.

When Greg reached the mayor's location, the crowd cheered.

Steve scanned the area and spotted some of the snow that had fallen earlier that day. His first thought was to gather enough snow to make a snowball and throw it directly into Greg's smug face. That would show him. He abandoned that thought though when he noticed Greg shake his leg. Steve followed the trail from Greg's leg to the ground where he saw Greg's foot. The big oaf had somehow gotten his foot entangled in the electrical cords supplying power to the tree. Steve quickly grabbed the cord that led behind the tree to where he was located and took up the slack until the cord was almost taut.

The mayor once again quieted the crowd. "As a wrestler, you're used to the count of three. So, we'll count from one to three, and on three, pull the lever." The mayor started the count, and the crowd immediately joined. "One, two, three."

Greg pulled the lever, and Steve simultaneously yanked hard on the cord. The lights flashed on. As the crowd cheered, the tug on Greg's foot unbalanced him. He would have remained upright, but the cord was still wrapped around Greg's foot. Steve yanked the cord again and trudged backward as if he were in a tug of war. The final tug was enough to topple Greg ... into the Christmas tree. Steve quickly retraced his steps behind the food and beverage stands, and several people rushed to the tree to steady it and prevent it from toppling as well.

A horrified gasp arose from the crowd, which was soon followed by laughter. The mayor's discombobulated look was enough to cause even more laughter. Unsure of what to do, the mayor simply shrugged and held out his arms, palms facing upward. "Well, what can you say?" the mayor quickly ad-libbed. "A wrestler's got to wrestle. I just didn't know his opponent would be our Christmas Tree. The mayor and the nearby carolers immediately began singing, *O Christmas Tree*, and the mayor urged the crowd to join in.

Austin was hungry and wanted to eat at one of the food trucks, but Greg was so embarrassed, all he wanted to do was leave immediately. Thankfully, Jennifer must have felt the same way and didn't raise a single objection to leaving.

As they made their way to the gate, several witnesses of the event made wrestling jokes similar to that of the mayor. One person even suggested that next year Greg dress as the Grinch if he wanted a rematch with the tree. All Greg could do was put on a smile that made him look constipated.

"At least you saved yourself some money by not having to buy food at the food truck," guffawed Jennifer.

"Can we stay a little longer?" whined Austin.

Greg shot him a glance.

"May we stay a little longer?" asked Austin, correcting his grammar. "We didn't even get dessert."

"I think your father got his just deserts for not liking Christmas," giggled Jennifer.

"Now's not the time to be an English teacher," Greg grumbled tartly.

Greg had certainly not regretted coming here with Jennifer. He wanted to remember every event, every second, save the Christmas Tree incident. That image would be burned into his mind permanently.

Having reached the sanctuary of the car, Greg was temporarily able to let go of his embarrassment. He relaxed in the peace of the moment and took in the crisp air, the clear night, the moonlight, the star-filled sky, the faint sounds of Christmas Carols emanating from the town, and the smell of evergreens blending in with baked goods.

Greg was tired after the long day, and he sensed Jennifer and Austin were as well. Austin fell asleep as soon as he was in the car. immediately. Jennifer found a station on the radio that played Christmas music, and she hummed along softly with the music. Greg didn't want to force a conversation, and he was content to listen to Jennifer's humming while trying to avoid staring at Jennifer. When the moonlight flooded the car just right, he could almost see a soft glow envelop her hair, at which point Greg was sure she was an angel. She was an angel to him anyway. Although he was tired, the ride back home ended way too soon, and he was disappointed when Jennifer turned her car into Stephanie's driveway.

Greg picked up Austin off the back seat and carried him into the house. Jennifer went along to open the door for him and to carry their door hanging.

"Let me put Austin in bed, and I'll be right back." Greg carried Austin up the stairs and disappeared while Jennifer stood in the living room. Greg returned in a matter of minutes. "Austin was sound asleep, and I didn't bother to wake him. Surprisingly, I had a really great time until the tree episode. I've had wrestlers jump me from behind but never a Christmas Tree."

"At least you're able to laugh about it now. I had a great time too. Maybe Ebenezer Grinchface is starting to like Christmas a little bit after all."

"Falling into the tree was really embarrassing. I don't know how that happened, but it serves as a reminder that Christmas and I don't mix."

Jennifer turned to leave. "Oh, here's your Christmas Fidget Coin you were never going to part with!" Jennifer handed him the coin, and their hands touched.

They stared intently into each other's eyes. Greg wanted to lean and kiss her, but she suddenly took her hand away.

"Good night." Jennifer turned to leave.

"Hey … uh … Austin has been talking nonstop about putting up a Christmas Tree. If you have some time tomorrow, we could use your help."

"Sure." Jennifer replied without a moment's hesitation. "Take an inventory of the Christmas decorations you have so we'll know whether or not to pick up more."

"Sounds like I have homework tonight," joked Greg.

"You do. I know you don't have a dog; so, you can't use the excuse that the dog ate your homework. And don't try another excuse. As a teacher, I've heard about every excuse there is."

"So, you've heard the one that I did my homework, but the Elf on the Shelf sent it to Santa Claus to evaluate?"

"I haven't heard that one; you get a gold star for originality, but you still better have it done."

"Yes, Ms. Christmas. And you can bring Kringle if you like. Austin really likes playing with him. I thought about giving him a dog as a Christmas present, but Stephanie would probably not be too happy."

"What? You've decided against the canned ham," grinned Jennifer facetiously. "No. She would not thank you for giving him a dog without asking her."

As Jennifer turned once more to the door, she smiled one last time and left. Greg hoped that the smile he had seen would be permanently imprinted on his mind. The rush of cold air came in briefly as Jennifer opened the door and vanished into the night. Within a few seconds, Greg heard Jennifer's car start and back out of the driveway. He stood silently staring at the door, rolling the fidget coin around his fingers and wondering why Jennifer backed away so suddenly when their hands touched. Greg stood there a full minute, relishing in the thoughts of the past several minutes.

Check Yes or No

Jennifer called Carol as soon as she backed out of the driveway of Stephanie's house. The phone rang and just when Jennifer thought it would go to voicemail, Carol answered.

"Hello," Carol yawned sleepily.

"I'm sorry. I didn't mean to wake you."

"No. It's fine. Is something wrong? Are you ok?" Carol seemed suddenly alert.

"Physically, yes."

"Did today not go well with Greg?"

"It was great," beamed Jennifer. "We had a wonderful day, better than I could have expected."

"That's good news, sis."

"I caught him staring at me several times."

"That's good too, unless it was a creepy, stalker kind of stare."

"It wasn't."

"Well, what's wrong? Something obviously is."

"I'm afraid that I'm giving mixed signals. He seems to like me, and I want him to know that I like him. I've not felt this way about anyone before. I just don't know how to play this game."

"Good gracious. Are you a fourth-grade teacher or a middle school student? Because it seems to me as though you're acting like a middle school student." Carol mimicked a middle school student. "I like him, but I can't act like I like him more than he likes me." Carol resumed talking in her normal voice. "What's next? Are you going to hand him a note saying, 'Do you like me; check yes or no?' You're an adult; you're not supposed to play a game with love."

"I didn't say that I was in love?"

"You don't have to. I can tell. Just be honest with him and stop acting as though you have a schoolgirl crush or that you're in a competition to see who can hold out the longest."

"It's probably silly of me to feel the way I do about him. He'll be leaving soon, and I probably won't see him anymore.

Plus, I barely know him. Is it weird for me to feel this way so soon?"

"The heart knows what it wants. As for the other, just enjoy the time you have. Just because you feel this way doesn't mean you have to end up marrying him. Take each moment as it comes and keep me informed."

"I haven't told you the whole story." Jennifer hesitated, wondering if she should mention Steve.

"That doesn't sound good. What happened?"

"Steve showed up." Jennifer waited to hear Carol's reaction, but no reaction came.

"I'm sorry," replied Carol. "Did you just say that Steve showed up? At the Christmas Festival."

"I did. He did."

"Well, I hope you didn't talk to him, or if you did, I hope you told him off."

"I think I showed my displeasure."

Carol played back Jennifer's comment in an annoying way that only a sister could. "You think you showed your displeasure. I would have shown him a fist in the mouth. No, make that the nose. The mouth might hurt my hand."

"He said he was sorry, that he really missed me, and that we should give our relationship another try."

"Of course, he said that." Carol now sounded angry. "He thinks your gullible enough to actually believe his malarky."

"If it's a contest between Greg and Steve, Greg wins hands down. Actually, if it were a contest between a three-toed sloth and Steve, the sloth would win hands down."

"I'm just confused. Greg will be leaving, and Steve and I have had such a long history."

"History being the key word, sis. Take dad's advice and don't associate with Steve at all."

"How did my little sister become wiser than me?"

"You don't put yourself out there emotionally to others. You can't even seriously claim that you did with Steve. Now, I'm going back to bed, and tomorrow you're going to call me in the afternoon and tell me all about today." Carol hung up before Jennifer could say another word.

Posing with the Belt

The next morning Jennifer awoke at her usual time. Anxiety from the night before still lingered within her. Although she had been afraid that the day's events would keep her awake, she had gone to sleep as soon as she got into bed; she didn't even read any of the book she had taken with her to bed. She thought about calling Greg to see what time, or if, he still wanted her to come over to help decorate the Christmas Tree. Good grief, she thought to herself when she noticed the time. He'll think you are a love-sick puppy or a stalker if you call now. She didn't want to appear too anxious. That turned men off quicker than anything. She waited until ten a.m. to make the call. When Greg answered, she tried to be as nonchalant as possible. "Good morning, I was calling to see what time you wanted me to come over to help decorate or if you had changed your mind."

"Oh, no. I'm still … I mean … we are counting on you coming over as long as it's still ok with you. As far as the time, it's just whatever is convenient for you."

"Probably this afternoon."

"Is one o'clock too early? It does get dark rather early, and I know you want to get a good night's sleep to start off the school week."

"One o'clock is perfect," she replied.

"Yes. Austin is really excited about it. See you soon, Jen."

"Ok, bye." She was thrilled that he called her Jen again. Just that one small thing made her feel special.

Jennifer went into the garage and attic and hauled out some yard ornaments and extra decorations she had. Although the air was cool, she had worked up quite a sweat by the time she had everything packed tidily in her car. She checked the time and noticed that it was already eleven-thirty. She didn't want Greg to see her like this; so, she ran inside and took a shower. It took her another thirty minutes to decide what to wear. She wanted casual and comfortable but not old and raggedy looking. She finally put together a combination that she could work in without looking like a farmer who had been in the field all day. No sooner had she put on a little makeup and done a minimal amount of styling with her hair than she noticed the time ... twelve-thirty.

She took Kringle out to the car, and he jumped in, excited and ready to go. Jennifer drove past the few houses between her house and Stephanie's house. Greg was waiting on the porch when she drove into the driveway.

"I knew you would arrive early, he exclaimed, smiling, as Jennifer got out of her car. Austin came outside, and Kringle barked excitedly at the sight of him.

"I thought I would bring along a few yard ornaments so that you would have something both outside and inside."

Greg took stock of the inside of the car. "Wow! You must have a never-ending supply of Christmas decorations."

"There are more in the trunk. I'll put up the yard decorations so that you don't have to worry about your knee. I knew that would be your excuse if I asked you if I could bring them."

"You're getting to know me too well! So, we don't have to go to a Christmas lot to buy the yard ornaments?"

"No. Those were in the garage! There aren't a lot, but they'll make the outside look a little Christmassy."

"That was thoughtful of you." Greg smiled, and Jennifer could feel the warmth radiate within her, melting any strongholds of resistance she had.

"Where do we start?" Greg continued as he rolled up his sleeves. "I'm sure Sergeant Christmas has a plan of attack already laid out."

"Well, I usually put the nativity scene in front. Those lights over there I use to line the driveway. I have lights to outline the front of the house, and then I put those yard ornaments near the house but far enough back that they don't detract from the nativity scene." Jennifer pointed using both arms at the various piles she had presorted.

Greg gave a quick salute and yelled over to Austin. "Private Austin, your help is needed PDQ."

"What does PDQ mean?" quizzed Austin.

"Pretty darn quick!"

Austin ran over PDQ, with Kringle playfully snapping at his heels.

Jennifer worked on the net lighting while Greg and Austin put up the yard decorations. Austin seemed to be having a great time. To Jennifer, Greg looked like a natural at being a father. She would have never guessed that he rarely saw Austin; the two got along extremely well. When she returned her attention to her work, she noticed that Kringle had pulled one set of net lighting off a shrub. She started to scold him, but perhaps he thought he was helping. She heard laughter and glanced back to see Greg pointing at Kringle. Both he and Austin were laughing.

They finished the job in a few hours. Jennifer was amazed by two things. The first was how fast Greg worked. The second was that even though he worked quickly, he involved Austin and took enough time that Austin really enjoyed helping decorate. "I hope these are enough decorations for outside. She wondered why she had even made that statement. For Greg, one would have been enough. She had her work cut out for her if she was to get him even a quarter as excited about Christmas as she was. On second thought, maybe a tenth would be more accurate. She thought about the Christmas play the kids were going to perform and how Greg's feelings about Christmas were like those of the protagonist in the play. She didn't want to change Greg; she just hoped that he would eventually get the Christmas spirit on his own. Christmas was about more than decorations and presents. It was about family, and she could tell that family mattered to Greg, even if those feelings were buried deeply within him.

"These are plenty. I've gotten more of a workout than in a wrestling match."

"You get a gold star for your work today," joked Jennifer. How is your knee?"

"It's fine. I'll still continue with the physical therapy, but I can tell it's made a big difference."

After all the decorations had been set up, she stood back and admired their work. She hoped Greg felt that way. She was pretty sure Austin did.

Now, they needed the Christmas Tree; so, they went to the same lot they had gone to when they picked out Jennifer's tree. At the Christmas Tree lot, Austin's first three picks were the biggest trees in the lot.

"If we pick trees that big, we'll have to put them outside and decorate them," informed Greg.

"Hey. That's a good idea," resounded Austin. "We could get two trees, one for outside and one for inside!"

Jennifer came to Greg's rescue. "These trees don't have roots. They'll dry up and drop all their needles before Christmas. Your mom might not appreciate coming home to a dried-up Christmas Tree."

"I didn't think about that. I guess that's why you're the teacher and I'm the student."

"That's very astute of you," added Greg. "Keep that up and the school may promote you to teaching in the fifth grade next year."

Jennifer poked Greg in the ribs with her elbow. "Don't say ouch," she warned. "I may have to take back the gold star I gave you. I've heard that one about being promoted to teach in a higher grade over a hundred times."

"Do we have a gold star for the tree?"

"We don't even have a tree yet, buddy. I mean Sparky."

Jennifer grew excited. "I think I may have remedied that situation." She ran over to a tree, followed closely by Greg and Austin. "How about this one? It's a scotch pine. They have excellent needle retention, which means less clean up when Stephanie gets back home."

"Is it big enough?" inquired Austin.

"It's perfect." Greg motioned to the same attendant who helped them when they picked out Jennifer's tree.

In short order, the attendant had taken down the tree and wrapped netting around it. "Do you need me to cut some off the bottom to fit your tree stand?"

"Uh. Greg winced. "Maybe."

"What kind of tree stand do you have?" asked the attendant.

Greg described the tree stand as best he could, making excessive use of his hands in the description as though he were describing a fish he had caught rather than a tree stand.

The attendant nodded as if knew exactly the type of stand Greg had. He started the chainsaw and within a few seconds cut off a length from the base of the tree. He carried the tree to the car and expertly tied it to the top.

When they reached Stephanie's house, Greg struggled with the knots, mumbling under his breath. Finally, he pulled out his pocketknife and cut the tree free of its restraints. Inside, Greg put the tree in the tree stand, and it fit perfectly. "That guy at the tree lot really knows what he's doing."

Jennifer beheld the ornaments and lights strewn across the living room floor.

Greg seemed to know what she was thinking. "I just brought everything in here that I could find that had to do with Christmas."

"I've got lights and decorations in the car if we need more. Well, I see you have both clear lights and multi-colored lights. Which do you want to use?"

"What do you think, Sparky?" asked Greg.

"May I show you something, dad?"

"Of course."

Austin ran upstairs. Greg could hear the noise coming from his bedroom and drawers opening and closing. A few moments later, he heard Austin's feet stomping down the stairs. Austin ran in carrying what appeared to be a photo album. "Promise you won't be mad?" Austin's face showed determination and hesitancy that alternated with his breathing.

"I promise. I'm not going to be mad at you."

Determination won out, and Austin flipped open a photo album that was bookmarked to a specific page. Austin turned the book around for his dad to see. The photo showed Greg and Stephanie when they were still married, along with a baby, in front of a Christmas Tree. Greg had not thought about that Christmas in years. He had forgotten about that photo until now. Stephanie's mom had taken the picture of the three of them at Austin's first Christmas. The tree was much smaller than the one that now stood before them. Greg and Stephanie were standing beside the tree looking down at Austin in Stephanie's arms. We looked so happy, Greg thought. Jennifer drifted over and took a look at the picture, and Greg noticed her smiling.

Greg bent down on one knee and looked into Austin's eyes. "Of course, I'm not mad. You don't ever have to be ashamed or fretful to acknowledge our past. Your mother and I were so happy when you came along. Just because your mother and I are no longer married doesn't mean the three of us are not still a family."

Jennifer bent over to look at Austin. "A lot of divorced parents don't get along after a divorce, but you have two parents who love you very much and have made it a point to get along with each other for your sake."

"So, what are you trying to tell us with that photo?" asked Greg.

"Mom always uses clear lights, but this photo shows multi-colored lights. I just wondered if we could decorate our tree with multi-colored lights this year."

Greg hugged Austin tightly. "You bet." A tear rolled down Greg's cheek, and he quickly wiped his cheek dry before letting go of Austin. "Do you have any other requests for the tree?

"Let's put popcorn around the tree," begged Austin. "I've never done that before."

"You got it." Greg found some popcorn in the kitchen pantry and popped several bags. He got the largest bowl he could find in the kitchen and dumped the popcorn into it.

There were still several unpopped bags remaining in case they needed more.

"We need a needle and thread to string the popcorn. Do either of you know where Stephanie might keep a sewing kit?"

"You mean we can't use glue?"

Greg shrugged his shoulders. He tried not to laugh when Austin asked about glue. Austin had seemed so serious, as though he was certain that everyone used glue. "I guess he gets that from me. Do you know where your mom keeps sewing materials?"

"No."

They spent several minutes looking for a sewing kit before Jennifer finally found it. She then showed Austin how to string the popcorn using a needle and thread. "Be careful to avoid pricking your finger. I only have so many band-aids."

Austin awkwardly began stringing the popcorn. "I've never stringed popcorn before. This is fun."

"It's strung, not *stringed*," Greg said, correcting him.

"Why can't all the grammar rules be the same?"

"I don't know. That's just the way it is. If I had to venture a guess though, I would say the reason is for people like Ms. Bell to have a job!" Greg successfully blocked another elbow thrown by Jennifer. Greg looked back to Austin to find him eating popcorn. "Just don't eat more than you're stringing for the tree."

"Why isn't it *strunging* instead of stringing?"

Greg looked over and smiled at Jennifer. "How do you deal with all of these questions all the time?"

Jennifer returned the smile and simply shrugged her shoulders.

Greg returned his attention to Austin. "Don't ask so many questions. Santa's watching, you know."

"Santa's just looking to see if you've been good or bad. I don't think grammar counts."

"It may if he's looking to see if you've been paying attention in school. Ms. Bell and I will start decorating the tree while you string the popcorn."

Greg's mind took him back to when he was a boy, younger than Austin. He remembered helping his parents decorate the

Christmas Tree. He only remembered them decorating the tree once or twice. They put up the Christmas Tree on Christmas Eve. It was an artificial tree. His dad said it was to save money. Because they put the tree up on Christmas Eve, decorating the tree was a rush job. Greg didn't think that they had a particular strategy for decorating other than to decorate as fast as they could. Greg grabbed a handful of tinsel. "What do you do with this stuff, just toss it?" He randomly threw tinsel on the tree.

"No. No. You don't do it like that." Jennifer picked off the tinsel that Greg had just tossed onto the tree. "It can't be all globbed up together in one spot."

"Is *globbed* even a word? Between you and Austin, I'm not going to be able to speak correct English by the time Stephanie gets back."

"Yes. It is a word." Jennifer gave a playful scowl before returning to her lecture on how to put tinsel on a tree. "You have to put a single strand of tinsel on each branch." Jennifer demonstrated the correct method of positioning tinsel on the tree.

"That will take forever." Greg took the tinsel and began to randomly throw it again on the tree.

"I think you need to let someone else do the artistic things?"

"That sounds like your patronizing teacher's voice." Greg tried to be humorous with that comment and hoped it had come out that way. If not, the day could take a turn for the worst. "You're supposed to be helping me like Christmas, you know."

"It's not patronizing. It's just a little nudge. Besides, I don't really care how you decorate the tree, but Stephanie might."

"You've got a good point there."

Austin tossed the popcorn strings to the side. Either he was finished, or he had had enough of that, thought Greg. Jennifer would probably string more popcorn if needed.

"Dad? Will you help me make a Christmas Card for mom?"

"I think Ms. Bell might think you would do better without my artistic abilities. Or lack of artistic abilities."

Jennifer squinched her eyes and wrinkled her nose as she looked at Greg. "Don't be such a grinch face." Then she turned to Austin. "I think your mom would appreciate any card you make for her." She turned back to face Greg, "but having your dad help will be a good way for you both to share the Christmas spirit. Both of you can work on the card. The tree is almost done. I'll just need to fix the tinsel," she added, looking at Greg.

"I don't know if we have everything we need to make the card." Austin had a worried look on his face.

"I keep plenty of things like construction paper, crayons, markers and the like in the trunk of my car. It's a hazard of my job."

Jennifer temporarily stopped decorating the tree to go to her car and look for the materials she had mentioned to Austin. Within a few minutes, she returned carrying two bags full of materials. Greg took them from her and went into the dining room so that they could have a space to spread out. Greg pulled out all of the materials and sorted them into like categories. Crayons, markers, glue, and glitter were spread out on the table. He thought Jennifer would at least be proud of his organizational skills. Austin selected a piece of heavy construction paper and carefully folded it in half.

After Austin had folded the paper in half, he seemed puzzled as to what to do next. "What should we put on the card?"

"I don't know. What do you think your mom would like?"

"Mom and I usually decorate the tree together. Well, mom does it mostly, but I help some. She's missing it this year."

"I'm sorry buddy," and he was. He didn't think such a simple thing would touch him, but it did.

Austin thought a while, and then a big smile spread across his face. "I think I'll make a card showing mom and me, and you too dad, all decorating the tree together. That way, she'll know that I was thinking about her, and maybe she won't miss it so badly."

Greg brushed Austin's hair with his hand and smiled at his thoughtful son. He must have inherited his thoughtfulness from his mom.

Austin looked up at Greg with big, questioning eyes. "Did you ever help mom decorate the Christmas Tree?"

Greg suddenly realized how insensitive he had been over the years. He felt like a cad, but he had to answer his son honestly, especially with Austin's eyes seemingly looking through him into his soul. "Not really. Just the one time you have the photo of." Greg had been having too much fun to let his spirits be dampened now. He willed himself to cheer up. "What you want to do is a wonderful idea. I think she'll really love it. What do you want me to do?"

"You can hand me the things I need, sort of like in an operating room. I'll say *red crayon*, and you can hand me the red crayon."

"I think even I can do that."

Over the next thirty minutes, Greg handed Austin different colors of crayons and glitter as Austin made the card. Austin examined the finished product with scrutinizing eyes. The card showed a decorated Christmas tree with three people standing together on one side of the tree. The people were labeled *Dad*, *Mom*, and *Austin*. Austin opened the card, and on the inside of the card he had written, *Merry Christmas, Mom. Next year, we will all decorate the tree together. Love, Austin*.

"Why don't you give your mom a call?"

Austin was excited as Greg gave him his phone to call his mother. As soon as Stephanie answered, Austin started telling her what they had done that day. Greg was certain that Stephanie was sad that she couldn't be there to participate, but he knew she would have been more upset had she not gotten the chance to talk with Austin. They talked for about fifteen minutes. Greg was afraid that Austin would become sad after a while, having missed doing those things with his mom, but he still seemed excited when the call ended.

With the Christmas Card and the call to Stephanie completed, Greg and Austin went back into the living room to check on Jennifer's progress. The Christmas Tree was completely decorated. Jennifer was inspecting the decorations.

Greg was amazed at how beautiful the tree looked. He was also amazed at how beautiful Jennifer looked as she was finishing her inspection. The ugly Christmas sweater she wore with her sweatpants made him feel like he was finally at home, at peace, and this was his family. "That's a beautiful tree. You outdid yourself."

"It's beautiful," echoed Austin. "Do you want to see the Christmas Card we made for mom, Ms. Bell?"

"I'd love to."

With pride showing on his face, Austin showed her the card.

"That's a lovely card. Your mom is going to be so excited to see it."

"Do you think so?" asked Austin for more validation.

"I know so. I didn't know you were so talented. I'll have to get your help with the next bulletin board."

"Ok. Let's see what this tree looks like once it's lit." Greg found the end of the cord and plugged it into the outlet. Light burst forth, illuminating the tree with multi-colored lights that reflected off the tinsel to create even richer colors.

All three stood back and admired the tree. Jennifer was on Greg's left and Austin was on his right. He put his arms around Jennifer and Austin, and both leaned in toward Greg. He was happier than he had felt in a long time, like he was part of a family again.

Greg didn't want this moment to end, but he knew it was close to Austin's bedtime. "Austin, I think it's time for you to go to bed. Say goodnight to Ms. Bell and go get ready for bed. I'll be up a little later to say goodnight."

"Aw, come on, dad. It's not that late yet. Let me stay up a little longer."

Greg picked Austin up and pretended to wrestle with him. "I think someone thinks they're going to beat the world champion."

Jennifer came over and grabbed Greg, pretending to wrestle as well. "I think Austin needs some help."

"Double-teaming me, huh? What's your Christmas name again?" he asked Jennifer.

Jennifer had a curious look on her face as she answered. "Tickle Me McJingletoes."

Greg immediately put Austin down from high atop his head, and Austin ran out of the room laughing. Greg turned to Jennifer and began tickling her. "You said to tickle you."

Jennifer laughed as Greg tickled her. "Ok. Stop."

Greg stopped tickling her. Their faces were close together, and they stared into each other's eyes. Greg could feel the excitement coursing through his body. He could see the desire on Jennifer's face, and it pulled him to her like a magnet. Or was it those beautiful hazel eyes that bore into his soul that pulled him in? They both leaned in, putting their arms around each other. Mouths parted in eager expectation. Their lips almost touched, but the kiss eluded them both as Austin ran back into the room playfully yelling, "Ah!"

Austin ran into them both, and Greg fell backward onto the couch, still holding Jennifer. She landed on top of him. Jennifer's hair dangled teasingly a few centimeters over his face until several strands brushed softly onto his welcoming face. Her hair was soft and smelled like a fresh snow. Her warm breath gently caressed his face. Again, they stared into each other's eyes, oblivious to Austin, who pretended to be a wrestling referee. Greg's thoughts were interrupted as he heard a count, and for a split second he was back in the wrestling ring. His muscle memory told him to kick out, but as he looked into Jennifer's eyes, the last thing he wanted to do was move.

"One. Two. Three," counted Austin. "The winner, and new world champion, is Ms. Bell!" Austin held her arm in the air in victory as the winner.

Greg's full attention returned to Austin. "Hey! That's not fair. There was outside interference."

"Too bad, dad. You lost. Ms. Bell is the champion now." A mischievous look appeared on Austin's face. "So, Ms. Bell, since you are the new world champion, may I stay up a little later?" Greg could see the pleading in Austin's eyes, and he would have succumbed to the request.

"I'm sorry, but I want to keep my title a little longer," she laughed. "So, I'd better not go against your dad. Time for you to go to bed."

Austin moaned. "Aw. Oh, well. It was worth a try. Goodnight, Ms. Bell."

"Wait just one minute, son. I want to see something."

Jennifer and Austin looked at each other, and Greg knew they were wondering what he was up to. Greg went to the guest room where he was staying and pulled out the world wrestling championship belt from the dresser drawer. People would probably think he was crazy for having it with him, but he didn't really know of a safer place where he would have quick access to it. He had already had to wear it when he went to Louisville. He put it behind his back once he got to the bottom of the stairs. Before he went into the living room, he asked both Jennifer and Austin to close their eyes. He emphasized for them not to peek. Greg positioned himself behind Jennifer, asked her to hold her arms out, and to trust him. She did as he asked, and Greg quickly slipped the wrestling belt around her and fastened it. Even at the tightest setting, the belt would have fallen off of her had he not held it in place.

When Jennifer opened her eyes, Greg thought that she looked like a kid on Christmas Day who had gotten exactly what she wanted from Santa Claus. As Greg held the belt, Jennifer made several poses. She held up her arms to show her biceps, and Austin laughed. Greg asked her to hold on to the belt. Once she grabbed the belt to keep it from falling to the floor. Greg grabbed his phone and snapped several pictures of Jennifer with the belt. She didn't seem embarrassed when he took the pictures. She seemed to really enjoy it.

"I've never worn the belt," sighed Austin.

Greg thought back and realized that Austin was right. A pang of regret gnawed at him for never letting Austin hold it. "We'll remedy that." Greg placed the belt over Austin's shoulder and took several more pictures with Austin showing off the various poses he had seen on television. After a few minutes, Greg took the belt back and handed it to Jennifer.

Without needing to be told, Austin smiled and turned to go upstairs to bed. Good night, dad. Good night, Ms. Bell."

"Good night, Sparky," bid Greg.

"I suppose I'd better go," declared Jennifer. "Good night, Austin."

Greg thought that even Jennifer's voice sounded like an angelic benediction. Greg heard Austin thumping up the stairs on his way to his bedroom. Austin had a lot of excitement, and Greg hoped that Austin wouldn't have trouble falling asleep.

Greg turned to Jennifer. "I'm … we're glad you came. Decorating was so much more fun. with you being here." Greg knew that this day was for Austin. He thought he should feel guilty for thinking about Jennifer, but he couldn't help himself. "Do you really need to go? Won't you stay a little longer?"

"I'd love to, but I think I should go home. I have some things to finish up for school tomorrow."

"You know … we didn't really have a proper meal. Why don't you come over tomorrow night, and I'll fix dinner? It will be my way of thanking you for helping decorate."

"That's not necessary," replied Jennifer. "Remember, I've already heard about your cooking!"

"I'm getting better … slowly. Besides, practice makes perfect. What do you say, Silver Bell?"

"Why did you call me that?" asked Jennifer.

"I don't know. It just seems to fit."

"You just have endless ways of making fun of my last name, don't you? Ok, I'll come over tomorrow night."

"Great," smiled Greg.

Once Jennifer was outside, she smiled thinking about the names Greg had called her. Although she teased Greg about making fun of her last name, she secretly enjoyed it. Pet names were endearing, and something like *silver bell* was certainly more original than *sugar* or *honey*. She also liked it when Greg called her Jen. Although everyone called her Jennifer now, she remembered when she was a child, and her parents called her Jen. Hearing Greg call her by that name made her feel special. It was now a name reserved for him to use. She wondered what a good nickname for Greg would be, but she couldn't think of one. That would be something she would have to work on.

After he tucked Austin in and told him good night one more time, he went into his room and pulled up the photos of Jennifer wearing the world championship wrestling belt and exhibiting various poses. He couldn't help but laugh. He sent the photos to Jennifer and hoped she would appreciate them as much as he had.

When Jennifer arrived home, she noticed the photos that Greg had sent to her of her wearing his belt. Her face broke into a smile at the sight of them. Normally, she would have been embarrassed by the various poses she had done with Greg's world championship belt. There was something comforting about Greg. She felt confident in his presence. Jennifer thought about what Carol had said. Carol was right; she did love Greg, even though she didn't want to admit it. Carol had also told her to tell Greg how she felt. She could end up very disappointed if Greg didn't feel the same way. Still, she was going to do it. She made up her mind. Tomorrow, she would tell Greg how she felt.

Greg had a difficult time going to sleep that night. He couldn't stop thinking about Jennifer. She had certainly won his heart. He couldn't get over how beautiful she was. She was the reason he was doing as many Christmas activities as he was. His feelings for her had only grown, and he knew he needed to tell her how he felt. Telling her could jeopardize their relationship, but it was a risk he knew he needed to take. Tomorrow, he would tell her how he felt.

An idea of a present for Jennifer came into his mind causing him to grow even more excited. As he had explained to Jennifer, he had never been much of a person to give thoughtful, personalized gifts. But buying something for Jennifer actually seemed fun.

Texting Trouble

After Greg dropped Austin off at school the next morning, he could hardly contain his excitement until stores opened for the day. The jewelry store in town carried the exact present he was looking for, a silver necklace with a silver bell pendant along with matching silver bell earrings. The jewelry store clerk asked if he wanted it wrapped. The *no* that came out of his mouth surprised him. Although the clerk would do a much better job of wrapping, he wanted to do it himself. Once he got home, he wrapped the gift three times before it was presentable enough to give to Jennifer.

After dinner that night, Greg didn't have to do too much convincing to get Jennifer to stay longer. Greg turned on the lights for the yard decorations, and Jennifer and he stood in the yard admiring the display. Several houses nearby had their lights on, and the neighborhood was aglow with the feeling and sights of Christmas. They looked at all of the Christmas decorations and how people decorated differently for Christmas. At one house, Christmas decorations filled the entire yard, and the decorations were synchronized to

Christmas music, which gently wafted across the street. As they strolled back to the porch, Greg asked Jennifer to have a seat, relax, and admire the lights, and he would be back momentarily.

Greg came out carrying two mugs of hot chocolate. "Here. This will warm you up a little."

"Marshmallows?"

"Of course," answered Greg.

"Where's Austin?"

"He's playing a video game. It's a wrestling game with me in it; so, I couldn't say no."

Jennifer smiled and took a sip of the hot chocolate.

The chair creaked in submission to Greg's muscular frame as he took a seat beside Jennifer. "I had a cup of hot chocolate last night and one tonight," remarked Greg. "It's funny. Before the hot chocolate at your house, I don't recall when the last time was that I had hot chocolate, probably over twenty years ago."

"If it's not too personal of a question, why do you not like Christmas?"

The question seemingly came out of left field to Greg. Jennifer had asked the question quickly, almost as if she wanted to get it out before she chickened out. Greg let out a sigh before he realized he had done so. He thought for a moment, and then answered. My mother left us on Christmas Eve when I was ten. My dad and I never really celebrated Christmas after that."

"I'm sorry to hear that." Jennifer's face slightly reddened and she turned her head slightly, avoiding Greg's direct gaze.

"I still remember every detail. My mom and I were supposed to make Christmas cookies on Christmas Eve. I was in the kitchen getting the cookie cutters, and she just left."

"That's why you didn't want to make Christmas cookies with Austin."

"I married Stephanie right after college and went almost immediately into professional wrestling. I had to travel constantly and was away most of the time. Stephanie left me on Christmas Day when I had to travel to get ready for a match. Now, I'm always traveling around Christmas, which helps me forget. So, you see, Christmastime and I just don't get along."

Jennifer was now looking directly at him. He could see the sorrow in her eyes. Jennifer really loved Christmas, and the thought that someone had a reason for avoiding it, probably caused her great sorrow. "Does your dad or mom still live in this area?"

"My dad died a few years after I graduated from college and never saw my wrestling career take off. My mom remarried a few years after she left us, and she now lives in Australia. I haven't seen her in years. Work is my family."

"Was what you said to the class about being nerdy when you were younger true?"

"Yes. I withdrew to myself when my mom left. I was shy, not popular, and was picked on a lot. Then I had a growth spurt around thirteen and was tall and lanky. I started working out, joined the football and wrestling teams and excelled in both. And I became popular. I learned that you can't count on family; you can only count on yourself. That's why I have to do whatever it takes to stay in the limelight."

"So, you don't really have a problem with Christmas necessarily. You just don't believe you can count on anyone other than yourself. Christmas is a time to spend with family, which reminds you that you can't count on people. What's going to happen though when you can no longer wrestle or can't get any movie roles?"

"I hope I don't have to find that out for a long time."

"I've found the opposite to be true." Greg noticed a blank expression on Jennifer's face, and she was staring directly in front of her with her eyes seemingly not focused on anything. "I can't count on people outside of my family, or even myself, for that matter. Family is the thing that keeps me going."

Greg bent forward, resting his forearms above his knees. "Are you referring to Steve and your decision not to pursue writing?"

"That pretty much nails it."

"Let me ask you a personal question, now. Do you regret not becoming a writer? Do you regret turning down the publishing offer?"

"I prefer not to think about it."

"You're deflecting," challenged Greg. "I should know. I do a lot of that myself."

"I really love teaching. It would be difficult for me to imagine not being a teacher now. It's become part of who I am. But do I regret turning down the offer all of those years ago? Yeah. I regret it. That's why I prefer not to talk or think about it."

"I'm going to get some more hot chocolate. Give me your mug, and I'll bring you some too." Greg took Jennifer's mug and went inside.

Hot chocolate was not the entire reason that Greg went inside. He was going to tell Jennifer how he felt, and getting the hot chocolate would give him time to focus on, and gather the courage for, what he wanted to do.

Jennifer was nervous. Her insides felt as though thousands of tiny stars were bursting, sending their energy in all directions. It wasn't Greg's cooking that was causing the sensation. Dinner had actually been good. No, what was causing Jennifer to want to crawl out of her own skin because it was all tingly was the resolve in her mind. When Greg came back outside. She was going to tell him about her feelings for him. That's all there was to it. If he didn't feel the same way, she would leave, dejected. But if he did … Jennifer was already imagining the kiss she would be sharing with Greg in about two minutes from now.

An irritating vibration brought Jennifer back to reality. What was that? She quickly realized that what she was hearing was the buzzing of a phone. She looked over and observed Greg's phone on the arm of his chair. The vibrations moved the phone close to the edge of the arm. Jennifer grabbed it just as it was about to fall on the floor. She hadn't meant to look at the phone, but she inadvertently noticed that the phone displayed a text from *AGENT*. The text read: *Showing the manuscript U sent to a publisher friend*. Just then, Greg appeared back outside with the hot chocolate.

"You sent my manuscript to your agent?" Jennifer tried to remain calm, but she noticed the displeasure within her voice.

"Yeah," replied Greg with a look of puzzlement on his face.

"You sent my manuscript to your agent without asking or without even telling me?" This time the displeasure in her voice had increased to ire. She noticed Greg's eyes migrate to his phone in her hand.

"Why do you have my phone?"

"So, I'm not supposed to hold your phone, which I kept from falling off the arm of the chair, by the way, but you can send my manuscript without my permission?"

Greg seemed baffled. "I thought you would appreciate it. You just told me how much you regretted turning down the publishing offer."

"You're just like Steve ... trying to control my life. At least he says he has changed. The knowledge that Greg had shared her manuscript with someone she didn't know created a hollow pit in Jennifer's stomach. It was as though an intruder had rummaged through her personal belongings, violating her privacy and leaving her feeling exposed. Why did the men she liked always try to make decisions for her? Why did they think they knew what was best for her? "I've got to go." Jennifer put down the phone and marched off the porch to her car, leaving Greg standing there still holding two mugs of steaming hot chocolate.

As Bad as Steve

Jennifer's face was flush, heated by her anger. She wanted to talk with someone who would either validate her concerns or calm her. The only person she knew she could talk to about this was Carol. Using the car's Bluetooth, she called her sister.

Carol answered on the first ring. "Hi sis. How did decorating go today?"

"Everything was great until just a few moments ago. He's as bad as Steve was."

"Ooh, touchy, are we? First, I'm sure he's not as bad as Steve. Second, you said *Steve was*. I think it's *Steve is*."

Carol always knew the right buttons to push. Of course, she had had a lifetime of figuring out Jennifer's buttons and the best way to push them. It was almost as if she got joy out of poking the bear. "Greg gave my manuscript to his agent to try to help me get it published."

"So? What's wrong with that?"

Poke the bear a little harder, why don't you? "What do you mean what's wrong with that?" She could feel the hair on her arms standing up. "That's something I should do on my own!"

"Greg had enough confidence in you and your writing that he took a chance. Greg is trying to help you become a writer; Steve was trying to prevent you from becoming a writer. Greg was trying to give you options. Steve took away options."

Carol's logic and the calm matter-of-factness in her voice only served to agitate Jennifer further.

"Ugh!" Jennifer momentarily forgot she was driving and tugged the sides of her hair in frustration. She quickly grabbed the steering wheel when the car began to drift. "Whose side are you on?"

"Yours, obviously. That's why I'm trying to get you to put this into perspective. Was Greg wrong in not asking you first? Yes. So, you tell him it was wrong and to never do that again."

Jennifer couldn't argue with Carol's logic or her advice. Still, she wanted to be mad, and she was going to be mad.

It's Not over until the Bell Rings

Greg was thinking about the previous night as he waited in Stephanie's SUV to pick up Austin from school. It had been a wonderful day. He and Jennifer had seemed to be building a relationship. He was even feeling better about Christmas. But then, as things always seemed to do around this time of year, his hope was shattered in one moment. "You can only count on yourself." Now, he was talking to himself out loud. But it was true, and maybe he needed to hear himself say it.

Just then, the door opened, and Austin climbed in, bubbling with excitement. "Guess what, dad? I got picked to be on one of the Candy Cane Relay teams."

"That's great news. Your hard work and practice paid off." What he said sounded half-hearted, and Greg was disappointed that he didn't sound more enthused.

"I thought you were going to come and watch rehearsal for the Christmas play today?"

"I'm sorry. Ms. Bell is mad at me, and I thought it would be better if I didn't come by today."

"Well, you have to come on Wednesday. That's when the school's Christmas activities take place, including the Candy Cane Relay."

Jennifer's family was over that night for dinner, and they were eating the daily special from the diner.

"So, how is everything going with you and the wrestler? Did you patch things up after last night?" asked Carol.

"You know his name is Greg. You're just trying to get a rise out of me."

"That's what sisters are for. So, how's it going with **Greg**?"

"You two quit acting like teenagers," ordered Emily. "We thought we were through with all of that. And what happened with Greg to make you mad at him?"

Before Jennifer could answer, Carol butted in. "Greg showed her manuscript to his agent to see if he could help her get it published."

"Jennifer can speak for herself," warned Emily.

"Well, that was a lapse of judgment on his part, but you tell him so and move on," advised Coach Bell.

"He'll be leaving soon; so, it doesn't matter," sulked Jennifer.

"It's not over until the bell rings," chimed Carol.

Jennifer knitted her eyebrows and scowled at Carol. "That's not the way that saying goes."

"Yeah, but it works well since **Greg** is a wrestler."

"He's just like Steve was … controlling and gone all the time. And I think Steve has changed. He called me and wants to go out this week."

Coach Bell, who was just about to put a forkful of food into his mouth, set the fork down. "Steer clear of Steve. He lost his fiancée and his job. He's just trying to get back to the way things were."

"I think he really may have changed," considered Jennifer wistfully.

Third Row, Second Seat from the Back

Wednesday morning, Greg went to the door of Jennifer's classroom and stuck his head in the doorway. The room was unusually quiet, and he saw the students writing away in notebooks. He hoped he wasn't interrupting a test. Jennifer noticed his head in the doorway and casually made her way to the door and out into the hallway. Greg was nervous. Jennifer was quiet, which made him even more nervous. He pulled out the fidget coin Jennifer had given him and made good use of it. Looking around he noticed several holiday-themed bulletin boards on the walls in the hallway. Since Jennifer apparently wasn't going to speak first, he swallowed the knot in his throat and began. "I'll be at the school events this afternoon, but I wanted to apologize to you first. I shouldn't have sent in your manuscript. I realize that was wrong of me even if I had good intentions. I don't like the way things have been between us since the other night. Can you forgive me?"

"I was upset, but I'm over it. You're forgiven."

The matter-of-factness in Jennifer's voice caused Greg to doubt that she truly was over it, but he plowed on. "That makes me feel so much better." Not sure of what to say next, he said the first thing that came into his mind. "Why are the kids so quiet?"

"They're journaling."

"What's that?"

"I give them different topics to write about in their journals. Sometimes, the journaling activity is about what they're feeling. That's how I tell if kids are struggling sometimes. Other times, they journal before a test. Research has shown that writing about how you feel about a test can help reduce testing anxiety. Other times, I ask them to journal about upcoming holidays. That's what this journaling activity is about. I asked them to write about what they want for Christmas and what their ideal Christmas would be like."

"That's a neat idea. Is that something you did growing up?"

"Yes. I used to write in a journal almost every day."

Greg was running out of things to say, and Jennifer still seemed mildly agitated. He decided to end the conversation and hope for better things in the afternoon, now that the ice was hopefully broken between them. "I'll see you shortly at the events, Silver Bell."

The bell rang, signaling the end of the period, and Jennifer went back inside her classroom. Children were soon entering the hallway in droves. Greg turned to walk away and reached Helen's door just as she was stepping out. Jennifer came to her own doorway just in time to witness Helen colliding into Greg.

"Greg, I thought I heard your manly voice in the hallway. I'm still waiting for that cup of coffee you promised me."

Helen wasn't being discreet by any means. Several of the children snickered as they scurried past Greg and Ms. Collins. Jennifer reluctantly pulled her head back into her classroom before they could see her spying. She could hear their voices, especially Helen's. She could hear what Helen was saying but could not distinctly hear Greg.

"I don't remember promising …"

Helen interrupted Greg in midsentence. "Men can be so forgetful sometimes. Don't make me wait much longer. Santa's watching, you know. You might get a lump of coal in your stocking this year."

Children began entering the classroom, and Jennifer could no longer make out what either Helen or Greg were saying. Jennifer peered into the hallway once again and observed Helen smiling and acting giddily. She saw Helen and Greg talking, but the noise still drowned out what they were saying.

"So, Austin is in your class for math and science. How's he doing?" asked Greg. "Is he having any problems?"

Helen pulled a boy to her who was standing at the door. "Oh, Austin is doing fine. Right, Austin?"

"That's not Austin. Do you not know their names yet?"

"Oh, I memorize where they sit. Austin is in row three, the second seat from the back," said Helen.

"So, you know Austin's chair," exclaimed Greg.

Helen showed a silly-looking smile and nodded her head vigorously.

Jennifer still couldn't hear what was being said, but she noticed that Helen seemed impressed with herself. He must have asked her out, thought Jennifer. Jennifer pulled herself back into her classroom once more. I'm doing exactly what Carol criticized me for, acting like a middle school student with a crush. I guess Helen has won again. Well, he can have her.

Ho, Ho, Ho is It?

Soon, the children would be entering the gym for the school's Christmas events. At present, they were outside doing a Christmas-themed scavenger hunt, overseen by several teachers and several parents who had volunteered to help. Jennifer performed some last-minute inspections. She always looked forward to these events, but the drama between Greg and her had sapped some of her enthusiasm.

Greg had gone to the gym after his conversation with Helen and helped the other teachers and staff set up tables. They only set out a few chairs. One of the teachers said that those were for the adults; the kids wouldn't bother sitting.

Several of the teachers and staff began putting out plates of Christmas cookies on a few of the tables. Jennifer had brought several Christmas-themed aprons for the servers. One had a picture of a gingerbread man with the words, *Oh, Snap*. Another had a picture of a green elf outfit with stockings and elf shoes. Jennifer wore her favorite red Christmas apron that said, *I Just Want To Bake Stuff And Watch Christmas Movies*.

"That's a lot of cookies," marveled Greg as he surveyed the lineup. "How many are there?"

"I'm not sure," replied Jennifer. "Each teacher is supposed to bring thirty, but some teachers always forget."

"So, let me guess, you made more than thirty to make up for those who didn't bring any. And you didn't buy them; you baked them."

"Of course."

"How many cans of dough did you buy?"

"What is it with you and cans?" teased Jennifer. "First, it was canned hams; now, it's canned dough. I made mine from scratch."

"Of course, Ms. Christmas did! You're really going to give kids cookies so they can be sent hyped up home to their parents?"

"It's good to give the parents a preview of what's to come for Christmas," smiled Jennifer. "I suppose we can always give some to Santa, and then there are his reindeer." Jennifer tilted her head and focused her eyes upward as though she were in deep concentration, as she named off reindeer, "Dasher, Dancer, Prancer, Vixen, Comet, Cupid, Donner, Blitzen, Rudolph, and of course, Solicitor!"

The name of the last reindeer brought a chuckle from Greg.

"Hye, Greg," called one of the teachers. "Would you mind putting up one more table?"

Greg had just finished putting up the last table when Helen swished in and strode over to Greg. This woman just doesn't give up, he thought. Helen put her hands on Greg's arm, and he noticed that she had changed clothes. Helen was wearing a Hunter Savage collectible wrestling shirt that had been hand-decorated with gold garland for Christmas.

"Did you decorate that yourself, Helen?"

"Yes. Don't you just love it?"

"I have to say that you're quite talented." Greg told himself to shut up almost as soon as he commented. He certainly didn't want to encourage her.

Still holding on to Greg's arm as if it were the last pair of boots on sale in a department store, she batted her eyes and asked, "What do you get when you take the ratio of the circumference of a Christmas cookie to its diameter?" Not waiting for Greg to answer, she blurted out, "Christmas cookie pi. Get it? Pi, like in math." She laughed hysterically at her joke, still not letting go of Greg's arm.

Greg feigned a fake laugh. "Yeah. I get it." There was no emotion in his voice.

Helen laughed a little more and gradually let the laugh die down.

Greg observed her batting her eyes again. If she bats them any harder those fake eyelashes are going to come flying off as if they were reindeer taking off with a sled full of toys. As if batting her eyelashes and gripping his arm as if it were in a vice were not enough, next came the sultry voice. "Do you like the shirt I'm wearing? It's one of your collectible wrestling shirts that I decorated for Christmas."

Greg thought about saying that he had already commented on the shirt and her decorating, but he didn't want to appear rude. He wasn't sure what to say and settled with, "Yeah. That's nice."

"It's missing one thing." She looked at him as if she wanted him to guess, but he wasn't even going to try to guess what was in her mind; so, he kept quiet, waiting for her to answer.

"Your autograph, silly." She whipped a marker out of her pocket. "Here's a marker. You can sign it." She handed him the marker, purposely putting her hand into his, he thought. She finally released the marker and stood facing him, awaiting him to sign. He awkwardly tried to sign, and she thrust her chest out.

"Turn around. I think signing the back of the shirt will be easier." Was that a pout on her face? She seemed reluctant to turn around but eventually did. Greg signed the back of the shirt. He returned the marker to Helen who giddily strolled away. Greg was embarrassed and hoped that no one had seen this escapade of Helen's making. He ashamedly peered up to see if anyone was watching, and his heart almost stopped. No one had been paying any attention, except for one person, Jennifer. He couldn't tell whether she was jealous or angry; her face certainly didn't show amusement. Greg tried to hold up his arms in an *I don't know what that was* sign, but she looked at her phone before she saw it. Then, he heard Jennifer say, "Oh, no!"

Greg navigated to Jennifer. "What's wrong?" he asked. He was expecting her to say something along the lines of, *You know what's wrong. You've been over there flirting with Helen*, but she didn't. What she said caught him with surprise.

"My dad plays Santa Claus every year, but his back is out again." Greg could see the wheels turning in Jennifer's mind. "Would you play Santa for the kids this year?

Surprise was a mild word for what Greg felt when she asked him that. "Me? I can't …"

Jennifer interrupted his stammering. "Sure, you can. You're trying to be an actor. This will give you the perfect opportunity to put your acting skills to the test."

"But."

"No buts. He's still at the high school. I'll text him that you're coming over. You can run over and pick up his Santa suit before he goes home."

Greg didn't know if it was his guilt of Jennifer seeing him talking to Helen or if she was just that convincing with her teacher-voice, but he agreed to do it. Greg knew where the high school was, and he left immediately. Greg knew that Coach Bell was a teddy bear on the inside when it came to helping people, but he had a difficult time imagining Coach Bell as Santa Claus. The gruff voice alone would probably frighten children. He recognized the high school gym and went immediately there. He knew he was supposed to stop by the office and register himself, but he knew he needed to hurry.

Greg strode into the gym. Memories flooded his mind and took him back to his own high school days. He had been here a few times when his team wrestled against Coach Bell's team. He had a strange feeling of almost being home. The bleachers were tucked in, and he could see wrestling mats line the floor. The mats probably weren't the same ones he had wrestled on, but they were very similar. The gym was desolate, except for him and Coach Bell at the far end. Coach Bell had the stern look of a high school wrestling coach, and Greg still couldn't imagine him playing Santa Claus to a bunch of elementary school kids. As Greg got closer, he noticed the Santa suit on a hanger slung across Coach Bell's back.

"I'd pay anything to see you playing Santa," grinned Coach Bell. "You know … the school hasn't picked a new wrestling coach yet as my replacement. You would be great as a coach. If you want to do it, I'd put in a good word for you."

He hadn't done that kind of wrestling in years, and just because he was good at it didn't mean he knew anything about teaching others how. "Thanks. I appreciate that. I really do. It's a great offer, but I'm not quite ready to retire from what I'm doing yet." Aside from seeing Coach Bell from a distance a couple of times when he was in high school and seeing him again at Jennifer's house, he didn't know Coach Bell all that well, but he felt a connection with him. He didn't know why, and he felt as though he were letting him down.

"The limelight always fades, no matter who you are," replied Coach Bell. "It's pointless to try to hold on."

Greg felt as though Coach Bell could see him as he truly was: afraid to trust in others and keeping on the move so that he wouldn't have to think about it. "I'm afraid to let go." Greg couldn't believe he had opened up so easily to the coach. He rarely, if ever, did that with anyone.

"Only those who have no one to catch them are afraid to let go."

Greg didn't know what to say. The coach's profound statement hit home hard. He was amazed at the wisdom and quiet strength of the man.

"I knew it was a long shot, especially since you want to try your hand at acting, but it was worth a try. I hate not being able to play Santa this year. I've done it for twenty years. This was going to be my last year." The coach looked sorrowful. Then, he winced and put his hand to his lower back.

"Are you ok?"

"Yeah, I'll be alright. I just need to hold on until after the high school Christmas Dance tomorrow night. I have to be a chaperone."

Greg could not believe the words coming out of his mouth as he volunteered. "I'll do it for you. You need to rest your back as soon as possible."

"That's mighty nice of you, Greg. You'd better hurry now and get back to the school."

Melancholy cast a shadow of sadness over Greg's heart as he left the gym. This man that he barely knew had a lot of respect for him. When he met him at Jennifer's house, the coach had shown more enthusiasm for his wrestling ability than his own father had. The grizzled coach had a lot of heart. He really enjoyed what he did, whether it was coaching a bunch of high school know-it-alls or playing Santa to a bunch of kids.

When Greg arrived back at the elementary school, the suit was only covered by a see-through plastic covering as if it had just come from the dry cleaners. Fortunately, no kids were around to see him carrying it, and he quickly went inside a room behind the auditorium stage to change. He had just taken the suit out of its bag when he heard a knock on the door. "Ho, Ho, Ho is it?"

Greg was embarrassed at his play on words, saying *Ho* instead of *Who*.

"It's Jennifer," called the voice on the other side of the door. Greg opened the door and quickly motioned for her to come inside.

"I'm glad you're here. I need someone to make sure I get this on correctly."

"Well, I'm not going to stay in here while you change, but I'm sure Helen would be glad to help you."

Greg couldn't tell for sure, but he thought that was sarcasm. "If she's in here, I'll never get dressed." Greg watched Jennifer's eyes grow wide with astonishment, amazement, anger or some other emotion that he couldn't quite put his finger on. "I didn't mean it like that," he quickly clarified.

"Just how did you mean it?" snapped Jennifer.

Ah, the emotion was anger, thought Greg. "Just stay on the other side of the door, and when I'm dressed, make sure I look ok." He added, "Please."

"Very well. I just brought this by for you." She handed him some wearable padding. "I know you don't have the belly for Santa Claus."

"Good thinking. Your dad must have forgotten to pack that."

Once Greg got dressed, he opened the door for Jennifer to come in and inspect how he looked. She still looked annoyed, he thought. She inspected him, had him turn around, and then turn around once more facing her. She patted him a few times for good measure, he supposed. She gave him a thumbs up.

"The kids are ready for you. There is a chair for you to sit in."

Chair didn't begin to describe what Greg viewed as he went to sit down. It looked more like an ornate throne. Greg wished he could borrow this for wrestling. It would add quite the element to his world champion persona. The line of kids stretched to the end of the auditorium, which also made Greg feel like he was back in an arena awaiting a wrestling match. Several of the teachers took turns dressed as elves, taking pictures or handing out candy canes. Eventually, Jennifer took her turn dressed as an elf. He chuckled at seeing her wear pointy ears and rolled up elf shoes. She was the cutest elf he had ever seen. Occasionally, she would look over at him and smile with a twinkle in her eyes, the same eyes that had displayed anger earlier. He much more enjoyed seeing them twinkle, especially when looking at him. He hoped that meant she was no longer angry with him over Helen. It wasn't his fault anyway. He couldn't help how Helen acted, and he thought he had tried to discourage her as much as possible without being rude.

It seemed like he had been playing Santa for an hour, and there were still about half the number of kids as there were when he started. When it was Austin's turn to see Santa, Greg hoped that the disguise would fool him. He had been using a different voice and he tried to make doubly sure he was using this voice when Austin sat on his lap. "Hey, young man. What do you want for Christmas this year?"

Austin's request nearly floored him. "I want my dad to stay here and have Ms. Bell as his girlfriend." Austin's heart touching plea twisted Greg's stomach into knots and brought to light the dilemma that Greg had hidden in the recesses of his mind. Although he wanted to keep his relationship with Jennifer, he knew he would be leaving soon. But he couldn't give anything away now as Santa. He said the only thing he could think of. "That's a tall order, even for Santa Claus. No one can make two people love each other."

"Oh, you don't have to make them fall in love. They already are; they just don't know it yet."

"You seem very perceptive. Isn't there something else you want Santa to bring you?"

"No. That's all," and with that comment, Austin hopped off Santa's lap and scampered away, remembering to get his candy cane.

Greg's head was spinning as Austin's words sunk in. He was thinking about the words Austin had said, and he didn't notice Helen break in line. "Oof." Greg let out a startled noise as he was brought back to reality with Helen sitting on his lap. Before he could respond, Helen held a sprig of mistletoe over his head. She quickly leaned in and gave him a peck on the lips. "That's one thing I want from Santa this year." She rose and sashayed past Jennifer smiling. Greg saw Helen snatch a candy cane from Jennifer's clutched hand. The twinkle in Jennifer's eyes was gone. Greg hated to see the sad look on Jennifer's face. Why did Helen have to do that? Why did Jennifer have to have a bird's eye view? He had not even had the chance to kiss Jennifer, which he desperately wanted to do. Even Helen's peck on his lips was more than he had been able to receive from Jennifer.

The final activities for the afternoon were Christmas-themed games. As energetic as the children were at this point, Greg was certain that whoever came up with this idea as a release for their energy definitely deserved a Nobel Prize. The final game of the day was the Candy Cane Relay. It was an elimination competition. The last two teams were competing, with a total of eight children on each team. Four were on one side and four were on the other side. The distance separating

the sides was approximately fifteen yards. The person starting
the game had to walk the distance while balancing a candy
cane. Other kids could try to distract them, but there was a
boundary line the hecklers had to stay behind. When the child
made it to the other side, a transfer to a teammate took place.
This was a tricky part. If the candy cane dropped, the kid had
to go back and start over. If the transfer was successful, that
person would walk across the distance with the candy cane
where the next transfer took place. This pattern continued
until the last kid carried the candy cane across. This wasn't the
end of the game though. The final kid had to transfer eight
candy canes hooked together along a string spanning the
entire fifteen yards. Any candy cane dropped along the way
required the person to try again from the start. Austin was the
anchor for one of the two teams. Helen was cheerleading for
the other team, and Greg cheered for Austin's team. From the
start of the game until the midpoint, both teams were neck
and neck. At the midpoint mark, Austin's team started to fall
behind. Greg cheered as loudly as he could. On the last leg,
Austin carried the candy cane for his team. He started slightly
behind but caught up with and passed the other team's player
crossing the finish line first. But the game was still not over.
Two kids at opposite ends tautly stretched a string between

them. The opposing team did likewise. Austin was first to get his candy canes on the string, and he then took the string from his teammate. He began sliding the canes along. Now, the other team had their candy canes on their string and was trying to catch up to Austin. Austin remained cool under pressure and methodically eased the candy canes along the string while calling out to his teammate whether to raise or lower the string on the other end. As Austin's candy canes neared the end, the other team hurriedly tried to catch up, but a few candy canes dropped and broke on the floor. When Austin's candy canes reached the end, their team was declared the winner. All of Austin's teammates rushed Austin, celebrating and high fiving him.

Greg's heart filled with pride, not because Austin won but because his son, who had been struggling socially, had now succeeded and thrived in being a part of social situations. Greg looked around and noticed Jennifer standing near him, taking in Austin's success as well. As they caught each other's eyes, they both smiled as if knowingly passing a secret between them.

Greg started to walk over to Jennifer, but then his heart sank. Coming up behind Jennifer was Steve. Jennifer apparently saw the look on Greg's face and turned around just as Steve reached her. He hugged her and kissed her on the cheek.

Greg felt awkward standing there, looking down at his shoes and rolling the fidget coin around his fingers. He decided he could at least be mature enough to go over and speak to Steve.

"Sorry I'm late, babe," apologized Steve. "Since I've gotten my old job back, they've been keeping me really busy."

As Greg got near, Steve looked to Greg and simply said, "Greg."

"Steve," replied Greg in like manner. "Looks like you guys are back together."

Greg noticed that Jennifer started to speak, but Steve interrupted and answered. "We are." He put his arm around Jennifer's waist. "Jennifer wanted to go to the diner tonight. They're having Christmas Carol Bingo."

Something akin to a cross between insecurity and anger gnawed at Greg's heart, and he realized he was jealous of Steve.

He couldn't remember the last time he had been jealous over a relationship.

Suddenly, Helen dashed over. "Oh, that sounds like fun!"

"It does," remarked Greg mischievously. "Would you like to go, Helen?"

Greg thought Helen was going to do a cartwheel. "Really? Absolutely!"

Jennifer's mouth dropped open, but she quickly recovered. "What about Austin?"

"Tommy asked Austin to come over. Tommy's mother is here and said it would be fine. I just have to pick him up by 9:30."

Jennifer's mouth dropped open again. "Tommy McElroy asked if Austin could come over? Tommy is the one who was picking on Austin."

"Well, it's good they're friends now. Switching from enemies to friends and vice versa happens in wrestling all the time," stated Greg with little emotion in his voice.

Greg thought back about the relationship he had with Jennifer. It had seemed like a roller coaster ride from day one. He knew a lot of the dips were his fault, but he felt that just when they were getting close, Jennifer would pull away. Of course, maybe it seemed to her as if he were the one pulling away. With Steve back in the picture though, the roller coaster ride might be over.

Sir Gawain with Laryngitis

As Jennifer rode with Steve to the diner, she continued asking herself what she was doing. Why was she giving Steve a second chance? Was it because it had been a relationship she was used to? Carol had often told her that she didn't like to change. Was it because she had been mad at Greg when Steve called her? Was she doing it to make sure her relationship with Greg was severed? She felt strongly about Greg. She didn't want to admit it, but she was in love with Greg. So, why was she in the car with Steve? Why was she trying to sabotage what she had with Greg? But why did it matter? Greg was going on a date with Helen and had been flirting with her … well, actually, Helen had been flirting with Greg. And Greg would be leaving soon. Steve looked over to her, smiled, and patted her hand. She did her best to hide her inner turmoil. The questions and thoughts eventually evaporated from her mind, leaving only cobwebs of confusion.

Her mind was like a relentless prosecutor who would not leave her alone. No matter what she did, her thoughts boomeranged back to Greg. The outings with Greg were euphoric. Only a few days ago, she had told herself that this was the best prelude to Christmas she had ever had. She had been on an emotional high until that night she saw the text on Greg's phone. Deep down, she knew Carol was right. She should have scolded Greg and moved past it. Greg had sincerely apologized over the matter, and she had planned on calling Steve and canceling until she saw Helen with Greg. Why did she always let Helen get to her? She knew how Helen was. Greg had not acted on Helen's advances. He had done nothing wrong. Was she biased by Greg's wrestling persona of being a playboy? She knew he wasn't. At least, she didn't think he was. What did she really know about him? Or was she projecting her past boyfriend onto Greg? Well, they were similar when it came to work. Stop it, she told herself. This is someone you really like. Stop overanalyzing it and go with your heart. The battle that was raging within her was tiring her out.

"You're awfully quiet," said Steve. "Is anything wrong?"

"Huh? … oh … no … nothing is wrong."

As soon as they arrived at the diner, Steve had a phone call from work he had to take. Jennifer continued in by herself. She looked for Greg, but he wasn't there. She heard the door open and looked to see if it was Steve, but to her shock, it was Greg with Helen hanging on to his arm as though it was a pair of shoes she found at a holiday sale.

"It's almost time for Christmas Card Bingo," came the voice of the mayor over the microphone. "Everyone, get into pairs, and we'll begin in about ten minutes." The mayor apparently saw Greg, and he commented over the microphone, "Hunter, no wrestling Christmas Trees or anything else tonight." Several people laughed, and Greg gave a thumbs up.

Jennifer was standing nearby, and she heard Greg tell Helen he was going to get them some eggnogs. Helen asked for alcohol in hers, but Greg said he seriously doubted the diner had alcohol. When Greg walked away, she noticed Helen touching a necklace, a necklace identical to the one she had seen Greg buy at the Christmas market.

"Hi, Helen," Jennifer called to her over the noise in the diner as she walked up to her. That's a beautiful necklace. Did Greg give you that?"

"It's beautiful, isn't it?"

Greg returned with the eggnogs just as Steve walked in and over to Jennifer. Greg handed an eggnog to Helen. She took a sip and exclaimed, "I don't taste any alcohol in this."

"We're almost ready to start," announced the mayor over the microphone. "In this game, I'm going to call out a synonymous Christmas Carol title, and you have to correctly identify the Christmas Carol it references. I'll go around and pass out cards. Each team will play two cards. The first team to get one card with five in a row, a column, or diagonally will win. All phones must be put away. The mayor began distributing the cards. Some people ran to the bathroom. Some placed an order, and some just mentally got ready for the game.

About ten more minutes passed before the game finally started. The mayor repeated the instructions, and the game began. Jennifer and Steve were at a spot next to Greg and Helen.

"The first synonymous carol is *Sir Gawain with laryngitis*."

Greg scanned both cards and marked *Silent Night* on one of the bingo cards. "I'm really proud of Austin. He has made a lot of improvement socially and academically."

"I'm glad I could help," blustered Helen. "Of course, you've helped too."

"The next synonymous carol is Covert Observation of Matriarch's Scandalous Osculation."

"That's a toughie," mused Jennifer.

Greg marked *I saw mommy kissing Santa Claus* on the card.

Jennifer looked over as Greg marked his card. "You're pretty good at this," she told him.

"Brains and brawn are a good combination in a man," declared Helen.

Jennifer wrinkled her nose, as though she smelled bad fish, at Helen's comment.

"ABCDEFGHIJKMNOPQRSTUVWXYZ," exclaimed the bingo caller.

Greg marked, *The First Noel* on the card.

"How are you doing this?" asked Jennifer as she looked over again. "You're like a Christmas Carol ringer."

"I'm the best player in the game," he grinned. "You should be the ringer with a last name of *Bell*."

"The jokes with my last name never get old with you, do they?"

"Never."

A few more carols were called out, and Greg studied the bingo card. "We only need one more for bingo."

"Duodecimal enumeration of the passage of the Yuletide season" came the next carol over the microphone.

Helen called out, "Twelve Days of Christmas."

"If figures that a math person would get that one," asserted Jennifer, "but she gave it away to everyone else."

"We don't have that one on our card," complained Greg.

"Next is Sterling Carillon."

"Silver Bells," whispered Jennifer in an excited voice. The words brought to mind one of Greg's nicknames for her.

Greg marked it on the card. "Bingo."

Greg m the marched with the card up to the mayor, who carefully examined it before announcing, "We have a bingo." The mayor handed Greg a large stuffed Christmas Elf.

Some in the crowd cheered. Others wadded up their cards and threw them at Greg. "This reminds me of a wrestling match," he announced loudly to the laughter of the crowd.

Greg weaved his way back to the table. "Your prize m'lady," he bowed to Helen and handed it to her.

"It's so adorable!" gushed Helen.

Greg downed his eggnog, and he and Helen departed.

"I hate losing to that buffoon. That makes twice now."

"What do you mean?" Jennifer wore a curious expression on her face.

"Nothing. Let's go," urged Steve, and he grabbed Jennifer's arm tightly and all but dragged her out of the diner.

Once outside the diner, Steve let go of Jennifer's arm. She could tell he was fuming over the loss. It was just a bingo game, she thought to herself. All of a sudden, she blurted out,

"I decided to try to get my novels published." She didn't know why she blurted that out, especially to Steve.

"I thought we decided a long time ago that was a waste of time and that you were better off teaching."

Jennifer could hear the critical tone and edgy irritation in his voice. She put her hands on her hips, teacher-style, and gritted her teeth. "You haven't changed one bit. The only waste of time has been being with you. Don't call me anymore." She did an about face and marched back to the diner without glancing back once.

Inside the diner, she phoned Carol, who came to pick her up.

As Carol was driving Jennifer back to her car, Jennifer relayed the breakup with Steve. Carol let out a *whoop* sound and lifted both arms in the air. Jennifer had to reach over to grab the steering wheel to keep the car on the road.

"I've never been prouder of you than I am tonight, big sis!"

Silver Bell

Greg felt at least two generations out of place at the high school dance he had agreed to chaperone. The dance was held in a large commons area of the high school. Someone had put in a lot of effort in decking out the space for Christmas. It was a real classy look though. At least the suit he was wearing wasn't out of place at the dance. About the only thing that Greg was happy about at the moment was that the DJ was playing a variety of music.

As a song ended, the DJ announced, "We're going to slow it down for a few songs; so, grab that someone special for a slow dance." The song was one of those oldies but goldies 1950s tunes that was still good even today.

As Greg was enjoying the song, a flash of silver caught his eye. Jennifer was there in a beautiful silver dress. She was absolutely stunning. Greg felt as though he were floating on the song as it carried him like a river over to Jennifer. Before he knew it, he was standing next to her with no idea of how he had gotten there. Greg was in a sensory coma that allowed him to experience but not to speak. His eyes could not take in enough of the beautiful woman in front of him. Her shiny brownish auburn hair ended in a large curl that rested gently on her bare shoulders. Her hazel eyes set his heart on fire. The silver dress displayed her figure perfectly. When he thought his eyes could take no more, the scent of her perfume wafted in gentle waves over his nose. Although she had not yet spoken, his mind heard the angelic voice. Now, he needed, desperately wanted, to touch her, to kiss her beckoning lips, to put his hands on the small of her back. As the song was coming to an end, he willed himself to speak. "I know I'm the last person you want to see, but would you dance with me?"

"I'd love to." The angelic voice went through welcoming ears and bore its way to his head, burning a record in his mind that he would always remember.

Greg escorted Jennifer onto the dance floor. He laced her fingers in his left hand and put his right hand slightly below her mid-back. Greg cherished holding Jennifer close as they slow-danced. The touch of her bare skin that the dress teased sent him into ecstasy. As they swayed to the music, Jennifer laid her head against his chest, and Greg wondered if she felt his heart beating strongly. He could stay in this moment forever and be happy.

A part of Greg's mind needled him to talk to Jennifer while he had the chance. "My date with Helen was awful. I only asked her out to make you jealous."

Jennifer sighed. "My date with Steve was awful too. I broke up with him right afterwards."

The third slow song ended, and the DJ cranked up the tempo. Almost a minute passed before either Greg or Jennifer let go of the other. When they did, Coach Bell walked up.

"What are you doing here?" quizzed Greg. "I told you I would take your place chaperoning."

"You told him? I told dad I would take his place."

Both Greg and Jennifer glanced questioningly at Coach Bell.

Coach Bell shrugged his shoulders and the corners of his mouth turned down. "How else was I supposed to get both of you in the same place? I've got the rest of tonight. Why don't both of you go talk?"

"So, your back never was hurt?" asked Greg.

"Nope," came the brief response from Coach Bell.

"You're worse than mom at meddling," moaned Jennifer.

Greg and Jennifer ambled to the gym, silently. The gym doors had been locked for the dance, and Coach Bell gave the key to Greg. When they opened the doors, the gym was dark. Greg turned on the lights, and they strolled to one of the bleachers and sat.

"You look gorgeous, Silver Bell."

"Still making fun of my last name, are you?"

Jennifer gave half of a smile, and to Greg, her voice seemed to lack confidence. There seemed to be a sorrow that had replaced the tenderness he was used to hearing.

"It never gets old." Greg tried to remain upbeat in the throes of what his heart seemed to sense was coming. "May I ask you something?"

"Sure."

"I really care about you. Can we get past the bad parts? Do we have a future together?"

Jennifer sighed, as much with her eyes as with her voice. "I don't think so. I care for you deeply, but this can't work. You're the world wrestling champion. You're on the verge of landing a movie deal. You will travel all the time. I want someone to live everyday life with. I thrive on family; you don't. I love Christmas; you don't. We're too different. As much as I want it, this can't work."

"What if I said I would stay here?"

Jennifer reached out and took Greg's large hands into her smaller ones. "I don't want you resenting me for giving up your fame. You'll be gone soon and back in your routine. Let's just think of the good times we had."

With the last word spoken, Jennifer got up and walked out of the gym and out of Greg's life. The promise the night held earlier had now vanished along with the woman in the silver dress. A tear streaked down Greg's cheek as he pondered how many women he cared about had walked out of his life at Christmastime.

Greg, Buddy!

Stephanie arrived at the Cincinnati/Northern Kentucky International Airport around midmorning and took an Uber home. The flight from London to New York City was nonstop. She spent the night in New York and caught an early morning flight. Although she got a good night's sleep, she was still tired from the flight. As the Uber pulled up to Stephanie's house, she felt the most thankful she had felt in several weeks. To be back home, to spend the holidays with Austin was something she had looked forward to ever since she left. She pulled her luggage from the trunk and plodded up the driveway and steps to her home. Opening the door, she observed Greg folding laundry, which she thought was quite uncharacteristic of him. At sight of her, he jerked as if startled. The shirt he was folding floated out of his hands and fell into a lump on the floor.

"Hey, Steph." Greg had seemingly overcome his initial shock of seeing her walking into her house. "Welcome home." Greg spread his arms wide in a welcoming gesture. "Why didn't you tell me you were coming in? I would have picked you up at the airport. It would have given me another chance to drive the Porsche." She went over and let Greg hug her. "You know, I think it's time you traded your car. You have a nice job now. Get you a new one."

Stephanie's spied the Christmas decorations. Her head went from side to side and up and down. She spun around and noticed even more. "Somebody has been doing a lot of Christmas decorating." Next, she hurried toward the door as if she had left something there. She swung open the door to reveal the door decoration that Greg and Austin made. Her voice gushed with motherly pride, "This is perfect. Austin has been telling me all that you both have been doing. I wouldn't believe it if I weren't seeing it, but everything looks lovely."

"I know. It's uncharacteristic of me."

A sly look came over Stephanie's face, and she spoke as if she were a schoolgirl telling on her brother to their parents. "I hear that you've had someone help in changing your attitude toward Christmas and life in general."

"What do you mean?" Greg's intonation rose, and his eyebrows aided his face in displaying a questioning look.

"Don't play coy with me. Austin has told me all about you and Ms. Bell."

"You're not mad that it wasn't just Austin and me who did the decorating and Christmas activities?"

Stephanie walked over and grasped Greg's hand, palm in palm. Then she laid her other hand on top of his. "Not at all. She's a wonderful woman."

"She really is." Greg beamed.

You really do like her, don't you?" Noticing Greg's face and body language, the full awareness of just how much Greg liked Ms. Bell settled on Stephanie.

"It's more than like. I love her."

"You're in love with her?" Stephanie's eyes grew wide with surprise. She suspected strong feelings but was caught off guard when she heard *love*.

"I really am." Greg's smile was so wide, his teeth were showing along with crow's feet in the corners of his eyes.

"I couldn't be happier for you." She patted his shoulder, hoping that the subtle gesture would indicate to Greg that she genuinely was happy for him, but he suddenly appeared extremely sad.

"What's wrong?"

"I blew it Steph. I was coming around, starting to see Christmas in a different light. I had so much fun. I even believed it was a blessing for me that you went to London."

"You're using a lot of past tenses for your verbs."

"It's Christmas. Things never work out for me this time of the year."

"Granted, you've had some tough Christmases, and I'm sorry I left you on Christmas Day, but Christmas can be a time for miracles, for coming together too."

"For some."

She was about to say something when she heard a phone buzzing. Both of them turned their heads toward the end table next to the couch. Greg's phone vibrated against the wood.

He walked to the end table and picked up his phone. "It's my agent." His voice was neutral, and his finger hovered over the button as if it were a vulture waiting for its next meal. Finally, he jabbed his finger to the button.

Stephanie was acquainted with Greg's agent. He was fast-talking, persuasive, … and loud! She could easily hear him through Greg's phone as clearly as if Greg had turned on the speaker.

"Greg, buddy! The producer just called me. He apologized for taking so much time getting back to me, but they had a lot of auditions. They want you in the main role to play Allan Quartermain. The producer said that your physique, your popularity with wrestling fans, and your humor will sell the picture. Oh, he also said that you were a decent actor with lots of potential. It will really help if you wrestle at *Winter Frenzy* to keep up your popularity. They are going to start filming on January first in Africa. So, pack your bags, Greg, buddy!"

Greg pressed the button to end the call and turned to face Stephanie. Greg's face was pale, and he had a blank look in his eyes. Although she clearly heard Greg's agent, she was going to let Greg summarize the call.

"I got the part. They want me to wrestle the day after Christmas, and the movie starts filming in Africa on January first. I need to leave tomorrow."

Stephanie folded her arms and tapped her foot to an unknown rhythm. Her lips tightened, almost in a slight pucker. She wasn't sure whether to be angry with Greg or sorry for him, but anger was starting to win out. "So, you won't even be here to see Austin in the Christmas play." Her comment was more of a statement than a question since she suspected she already knew the answer. She huffed and shook her head.

"Come on, Steph. You know I've wanted this for a long time. Can't you be happy for me?" Greg spread his arms apart, hands out and palms up. Stephanie recognized this mannerism from previous occasions when he pleaded with her.

Stephanie responded sternly but calmly. "You have to do what you feel you must, but now that you've spent time with Austin, it's going to be hard on him seeing you leave. Austin can't wait another six months or more to see you again. I'm not mad, but I'm going to tell it like it is. It's not fair to Austin to come into his life and leave. You can't just drop in and out of his life." Greg's facial expression made him appear like a little boy who had been scolded. He even put his hands in his jean pockets and hung his head.

"I promise I'll see him more than I did before."

"I'm not the one to whom you need to make that promise. You talk a lot about the game. Austin's life is not a game. If you need a metaphor, I'll give you one. You need to ante up. Before you know it, Austin will be grown, and you'll look back and regret not being in his life. Kids grow up so fast. Before you know it, they're grown and gone. You don't want to miss this part of his life. It sets the stage for your future relationship with him when he's an adult."

"What do I do?" Greg's mopey eyes shifted to and away from Stephanie.

"You're an adult. Figure it out!"

Not the Coffee Date He Wanted

Greg had been on pins and needles waiting to hear this news. He had often pictured in his mind his reaction to the news. The picture did not match his current emotional state. He knew about left-brained and right-brained, but he felt as though he had two brains in his head. One wanted to pull a bent elbow and clenched fist backwards, the way that some football players did when they made a touchdown. The other wanted him to sit in a bar crying in his beer. Although he knew a person couldn't think two thoughts at the same time, he wondered if one could feel multiple emotions at once.

As Greg thought back about how he had treated Stephanie, shame confronted him like one of his wrestling opponents. He had treated Stephanie as though she were his mother. He had wanted her to decide for him. Stephanie was not going to accept that role. She called his bluff, as she often did, allowing him the opportunity to grow up. He sensed that he rarely did that though in Stephanie's eyes.

Greg was driving Stephanie's car, not knowing where he was headed. It seemed ironic that he was driving Stephanie's car and not the Porsche he had rented. He didn't know what that irony was, but he still sensed irony. He told Stephanie that he needed some time to think, and driving helped him think. Now, he wished he had taken the Porsche. When Greg noticed that he was driving into the elementary school parking lot, he clenched the steering wheel and sweat popped out on his face. He had to talk to Jennifer, but he also didn't want to. There were the two brains again. He hoped that the school gatekeeper in the office wouldn't let him pass. She did though, with a smile, a wave, and a gesture that she would sign him in. Greg skulked to Jennifer's classroom door. Peering into the class he saw a student at the front of the class with a poster board talking about the three branches of government. Shifting his attention to the rest of the class, he noticed that several kids had spotted him. More heads turned his way, calling attention to his presence. Jennifer finally noticed the turned heads of her students, and she turned her head to see what they were looking at.

Jennifer slowly rose from her chair, and Greg wondered if she was embarrassed that he was here, uninvited.

"What is it? I'm in class." She whispered. There was no greeting, no smile.

"I know." Greg bent his head in an apology. "I'm sorry to interrupt, but I have to tell you something. Can you meet me at four-thirty at the coffee shop?"

"Yes. See you then." Her response was terse, as if she didn't really want to talk with him. Before he could say anything else, she had already turned around and was headed back to her desk.

Greg tried to rationalize her behavior. She's in the middle of a class. She didn't know you were coming. The other brain told him a different story. She already told you the outcome of this at the dance. She has just been being nice to you; that's the kind of person she is.

Greg arrived at the coffee shop at four o'clock and paced back and forth while he waited for Jennifer. Every few minutes he checked his watch. He turned his head to the side, toward the parking lot at the end of the row of shops where Jennifer would probably park. He didn't hear the footsteps approaching from the opposite direction.

"Well, isn't this a coincidence?

He turned his head abruptly and was within inches of Helen Collins, who was carrying several shopping bags, almost more than she could handle.

"I wondered when you were going to have that coffee with me, and here you are."

Two shopping bags slipped through Helen's fingers and fell to the sidewalk. Both Helen and Greg stooped at the same time and slightly bumped heads. Helen laughed loudly, as loudly as she talked. Helen had stood up, but Greg was still bent-kneed. He picked up the two bags and handed them out to Helen for her to take, but she didn't take them. Instead, Greg was left holding them. She seemed mesmerized. Her eyes flashed and the corners of her mouth formed a sultry smile. She fidgeted with a necklace around her neck, gently tugging at it the way he sometimes tugged at his tie to let out heat. Greg stared at the necklace. It was identical to the one he bought for Austin to give to Stephanie.

Greg's eyes were wide, framed by arching eyebrows. The bottom of his jaw was slightly askew. "Where did you get your necklace? I bought one exactly like it for Austin to give to his mom."

Helen patted her necklace. "It's beautiful, isn't it. I saw it at a Christmas Market and had to have it." She was overacting in Greg's opinion. "Are you ready for that coffee?"

It's time I was honest with her, thought Greg. "Helen, I can't have coffee with you. I'm in love with someone else."

Helen dropped all pretense and spoke in a serious manner and tone to Greg for the first time. "It's Ms. Bell, isn't it? I could see it in both of your faces. She's a wonderful woman. You're lucky."

In speaking the last sentence, Helen's facial expression changed. The corners of her lips turned down, and the inner corners of her eyebrows raised. The sadness that showed on Helen's face stirred the empathy within Greg, and he wondered if this sadness was constantly lurking around her, hidden only by her flirtatiousness.

Helen reached up on her tiptoes and hugged Greg, putting her hands behind his neck to keep her balance. Greg returned her hug, hoping that it conveyed his thoughts of a newfound understanding and friendship. They let go of each other, and Helen's eyes were moist. Greg handed her the two shopping bags, and she slinked away.

Greg checked his watch again. It was after four-thirty. He searched the corner once more, hoping that Jennifer would appear.

❦

Jennifer left the school at four-fifteen. She could easily make the four-thirty meeting at the coffee shop with Greg. She feared she had made a grave mistake in ending their relationship last night after the high school Christmas Dance, and she had not helped improve matters today with her callous attitude when he showed up at her classroom. Why are you so stupid sometimes, Jennifer? She was her own worst enemy. I'm going to tell Greg I'm in love with him. I'm just going to do it before I chicken out. The fine hairs on her arm stood up from the electricity that pulsed through her; she was full of nervous excitement. She slammed the car in park before it came to a natural stop. Her key fob had slipped out of her purse and dropped to the floorboard. Her hands seemed useless as she tried to pick up the key fob, almost as if she were wearing mittens. Throwing her keys into her purse, she darted out of the car and dashed to the corner of the building, coming to a full stop when she caught sight of Greg and Helen standing in front of the coffee shop.

"I don't believe it," she mouthed almost inaudibly.

Helen had left school early, and a substitute teacher covered her last two periods. Jennifer's mind, in detective-like manner, put the pieces together. Greg and Helen had gone shopping, and they had just left the coffee shop. He was helping her carry her bags. Greg did like Helen; he was seeing both Helen and her. He was trying to have coffee with both of them, but the date with Helen ran over. This seemed consistent with Greg's wrestling playboy persona. In the YouTube video that Jennifer had watched, Greg, as Hunter, was accompanied by three flashy women. This was Greg's lifestyle. Even his wrestling name of *Hunter* should have told her this; he was a hunter of women.

Jennifer's heart dropped to her stomach at what she saw next. Helen was patting a necklace, the same necklace she wore at the Christmas Carol Bingo game, the same necklace Greg had bought at the Christmas Market. Greg had been looking at that necklace, and she saw him slip a necklace case into his pocket. When she asked him if he had bought anything, he said that he hadn't. Nausea swept through Jennifer, and she

thought she would actually vomit when she saw Greg and
Helen hugging each other. It wasn't a simple hug a friend
would give. Helen had wrapped her arms tightly around
Greg's neck, and Greg's arms wrapped around Helen with his
hands resting on Helen's lower back.

Jennifer's eyes welled with tears, and she could no longer
see the two. Dejected, she ran back to the parking lot and
climbed into the safety of her car. With her hands on the
steering wheel, she let her head fall into it. Heaving sobs shook
her entire body. Fearing that she might be seen by Helen or by
Greg, she straightened and wiped the tears from her eyes with
her shirtsleeve. All she could think about was getting out of
the parking lot as quickly as possible. The car squealed as she
sped out of the parking lot.

Pulling into her driveway, the nausea was still present.
Again, she threw the car into park before it had come to a
complete stop. She slung open the door and bent over. The
cool air outside was a blessing that transformed Jennifer's
shallow gasps for air to normal breaths. Unbuckling the
seatbelt and climbing out, she took one last deep breath of
crisp winter-like air through her nostrils, raised her slumped
shoulders and brought peace to her body. The peace was

exhaled as quickly as it had been inhaled. She plodded to the door and called Carol immediately upon entering her home. All she could say in her tear-chocked voice was, "Can you come over?"

Carol must have sensed her emotional state, and her reply was terse. "I'll be right there."

Dumb Ol' Wrestling

Greg added a jar of spaghetti sauce to the ground beef he cooked and drained the noodles in a colander. His body had gone through the motions of cooking, but his mind was elsewhere. He looked at his phone, which showed the time was six-thirty. He called Jennifer, but it rang until her voicemail answered. Even though he heard Jennifer's recorded voice, he drank it in.

"Hi. You've reached the voicemail of Jennifer Bell. I can't talk at the moment. Please leave a message at the beep."

"Jen, this makes call number four. I don't know if you forgot about meeting me or if something is wrong. Give me a call. Please. There is something important I really need to tell you."

After dinner, Greg, Stephanie, and Austin sat in the living room.

"I can't believe dad actually cooked a good meal."

"It was good," echoed Stephanie. She held up the Christmas Card that Austin made for her. "This is very beautiful, Austin. I love it."

Austin's face beamed. "Dad helped me with it. He was my assistant and handed me things when I called for them."

"I noticed that you put multi-colored lights on the Christmas tree."

"Dad said it was ok." Austin told her about the picture in the photo album of the three of them in front of the Christmas tree when he was a baby and that the lights on that tree were multi-colored.

Stephanie's facial expression was somewhere between sadness and concern, thought Greg. "I'm sorry, sweetie. I've never thought to ask you what color of lights you wanted on the tree. You know that you can always talk to me and tell me what you're feeling, don't you?"

"Yes, mom." Austin ran to his mother and hugged her.

Greg rubbed the back of his neck and then fidgeted with the Christmas Fidget Coin that Jennifer gave him. He glanced around the room and locked eyes on Stephanie and cleared his throat.

With her eyes still on Greg, Stephanie knew she needed to start the conversation. "Austin, sweetie, your dad needs to tell you something."

Greg put the fidget coin into his pocket, and with a determined look on his face, patted the cushion on the couch. "Come sit on the couch with me, son."

Austin moved from the floor and plopped onto the couch. Greg turned his body to face Austin and looked into his eyes. My agent called today to tell me that I have the leading role in the movie I auditioned for. I need to go back and get ready. I'll probably have a few matches before Christmas, but I'll definitely need to wrestle the day after Christmas at *Winter Frenzy*. Then, I have to go immediately afterwards to Africa because we start filming the first of January."

"You mean you won't be here to see me in the Christmas play, and you won't be here for Christmas?"

"I'm really sorry." Greg's eyes shifted away from Austin. "A movie role like this is something I've been wanting for a long time. It will bring in a lot of money, and I can help your mother pay off the house and set aside money for you to go to college."

Stephanie scowled and interrupted at this point. "I've told you. I don't need your help in paying off the house."

Stephanie had called his bluff again. He had tried to make leaving about them when it was really about him.

"I don't want you to go, dad." Austin choked back tears, and his voice grew whiny. "Haven't you enjoyed it here?"

"Of course, I have."

"Then why won't you stay?"

Greg interlaced his fingers and exhaled sharply through his nose. "You know I have to travel for wrestling, and you knew I had a shot at this big movie role. Don't you want to see your dad in the movies?" He poked Austin playfully in the side. "This is a great opportunity for me. Look, I promise that I won't wait as long to see you as I have in the past."

Tears streamed from droopy eyes down Austin's cheek and past his quivering mouth. "Did I do something wrong?"

Greg grabbed one of Austin's shoulders in each of his large hands and looked directly into his eyes. "No. I'm proud of you, son. I told you. It's work. Hey, I'll make it up to you. I'll get you lots of presents, and I'll send you something from Africa."

"I don't care about presents. All I want is you." Austin leapt off the couch and sprinted to his room, yelling at the top of his lungs, "I'm never going to watch dumb ol' wrestling ever again."

Greg heard the door slam and the creak of Austin's bed, and he let out a long sigh. "That didn't go well."

Stephanie strayed over and put her hand on Greg's shoulder. "He didn't mean it about wrestling. He'll watch, and he'll get over the other. It will just take some time. You just need to keep your promise to see him more often." Greg stared at his shoes and didn't comment on Stephanie's attempt to make him feel better. "What else is wrong? I can tell that something is bothering you, aside from leaving Austin."

"There is," Greg replied flatly.

"It's Ms. Bell, isn't it?"

"I went to the school and asked Jennifer if she would meet me at the coffee shop and that there was something I needed to tell her. Although she said she would meet me there, she never showed up. I called several times, but she never answered. I even left several messages." Greg scratched his head at the thought of the sequence of events.

"Something may have come up. You need to talk with her before you leave."

"You're right. I don't want to try calling her again though. Is it ok with you if I go over to her house?" Stephanie knew that Greg didn't like asking, especially since she just got back in town, but she knew he really wanted to get to the bottom of why Jennifer didn't show and why she wouldn't return his calls.

"I've got Austin. You just go and talk with her."

Greg thanked Stephanie and grabbed the car keys. Stephanie hugged him to try to reassure him. She knew that he was worried and that he hoped that nothing was wrong with Jennifer. Stephanie hoped she was fine, and that there had just been some miscommunication. If she were being honest with herself though, she knew that the night would end in heartbreak, and she truly felt sorry for Greg.

Do Me a Favor

The television in Jennifer's living room provided background noise as Jennifer explained what she witnessed to her family. Besides Carol, her parents were there as well. Jennifer preferred not hearing only her voice as she talked about uncomfortable situations; it somehow made her feel as if she weren't the sole focus of attention, even if she was. "He was outside the coffee shop where he said he would meet me, but he had been with Helen. They had been shopping, and he was carrying some of her bags. She was also wearing the necklace I saw him buy at the Christmas Market."

Coach Bell tried to help Jennifer remain positive. "It might not have been what it looked like."

Jennifer's arms shook from clinching her fists so tightly, and her neck muscles tensed. "They were hugging each other. Helen has flirted with him from day one. I guess she finally won out."

Carol rubbed her chin, and she stared at a corner of the ceiling. "Let's just think about this for a minute. It just doesn't make any sense. You two have spent almost every free moment with each other. I don't see how he could have had any time to spend with Helen."

Jennifer began talking over Carol before Carol had a chance to finish her sentence. "His ex-wife said he can't commit. I should have believed her. I guess this proves it. The one thing I hoped I'd learned from my last relationship was to pick a guy who would make a commitment to me. I never learn."

Greg's picture showed on the tv screen, catching the attention of both Jennifer and her parents. Jennifer increased the volume, and an attractive blonde spoke while Greg's picture was displayed in the corner of the screen. "Tonight's top story on Hollywood Headlines: Professional wrestler Hunter Savage is rumored to have landed the starring role of Allan Quartermain in the remake of *King Solomon's Mines*. The high-budget movie marks the first major acting role for Hunter Savage who follows in the footsteps of other wrestlers turned actors, such as Dwayne Johnson, John Cena, and Dave Bautista." Jennifer mashed the power button on the remote to turn off the tv.

Jennifer threw her hands in the air. "See? He hasn't even bothered to tell me he got the role."

"I'm so sorry. I thought you two were really good together. I still think you need to talk with him," encouraged Emily.

The doorbell rang, and Jennifer wanted to retreat further into the house. She didn't want anyone to see her like this. She looked on her phone and saw that Greg was standing at her door."

"I don't want to talk with him," she said through gritted teeth.

"I'll go talk with him," volunteered Coach Bell.

Greg was expecting, or at least hoping, that Jennifer would come to the door. Instead, the person who opened the door and wandered outside was Jennifer's dad. Coach Bell motioned for Greg to follow him, and Greg walked with him a short distance from the house.

"Sorry, son. She doesn't want to see you right now. Greg thought that the coach's gravelly voice held an empathetic tenderness, which also seemed mirrored in his eyes. Her dad genuinely seemed sorry. Of course, Greg expected him to take his daughter's side, but the coach seemed to be temporarily looking beyond family loyalties.

"I wanted to tell her I landed the movie role and see why she didn't meet me at the coffee shop?

"She knows about the movie; it just showed up on that Hollywood Headlines television show. And she saw you at the coffee shop with Helen and with bags in your hands."

Greg was totally confused. He felt like he was in a parallel universe. "Helen?" Greg felt baffled at just saying her name. He needed to set the record straight. He wondered what Coach Bell had to be thinking. "I wasn't …" Then it hit Greg, like an errant elbow to the head in one of his professional wrestling matches. "Oh …" The gravity of the situation settled fully on his mind and his emotion. Greg replayed the scene in his mind, and out loud for Coach Bell. "That explains it. Helen just came by from shopping while I was waiting for Jennifer." She dropped some bags, and I picked them up. We never had coffee together. And we definitely didn't go shopping together. I told Helen I love Jennifer."

Coach Bell stoked his chin, tilted his head slightly upward, and gazed upward with his eyes. Greg sensed that he was searching for the right words to say. "In professional wrestling and amateur wrestling, a referee only sees what he sees. Jennifer saw, and her mind filled in the details."

"I need to tell her what happened."

"There's more to it than that, and you know there is."

"Huh? What do you mean?" Greg knew he could clear everything up if he could just have the opportunity."

"Greg, let me be real and personal with you, if I may."

"Certainly. Go ahead."

"I don't want to be preachy. You know Jennifer is close with family, and as you might imagine, she's shared things with us. I know about your aversion to Christmas and about your family life. Not all families are as close as Jennifer's family, and not all families are like the one you experienced. I told you previously that at some point the limelight will eventually fade. When it does, you either have yourself or you have family. From your experience, I understand why you might choose yourself over family. From my experience, the key has always been a loving family. And as with anything, what you put into something is what you get out of it. You're at a pivotal point in your life, and only you can decide what you'll do. Please make the right choice."

Greg was not taken aback by the coach's words. Coach Bell seemed to genuinely care for his well-being, but he couldn't help but wonder why. Before he realized it, he vocalized his inner thoughts. "Why are you so kind to me?"

The corners of Coach Bell's mouth gradually turned up to form a smile, and his eyes almost seemed to twinkle. "When I saw you and Jennifer fifteen years ago, I just had an instinct that you two were a good match. A vision formed in my mind of you two together at some point. It was only there for an instant, but it was there."

Greg felt for sure he was in a parallel universe now. If he didn't know how sharp the coach was, he would have questioned the man's mental acuity. "What do you mean? I just recently met Jen."

Coach Bell smiled the widest smile he had ever seen on the man's face, and it displayed a sort of mischievous dance, as though it were hiding some long-held secret that could barely contain itself any longer. "Think back, if you can, to the regional wrestling championships in your senior year. Do you remember the match?"

Greg's head rose slightly as he searched his memory. "Yeah. I wrestled a guy named … Steve … Steve Ross, Jennifer's boyfriend! And I met this pretty girl … That was Jennifer!" Greg's insides tingled at the memory, and the realization of the recollection both renewed and strengthened his resolve to make things right with Jennifer. "I need to talk to her."

Coach Bell had already headed back to the door. He turned around at Greg's statement. "Give her a little time. She'll come around." Coach Bell hesitated as if trying to decide whether or not to say something in particular. "If you have time, you might do me a favor. In one of those cities you're going to, take some time and volunteer for a couple of hours. A lot of churches wrap angel tree presents for kids. It might give you a little perspective." And with that, he walked back into the house.

Greg had never really believed in the whole *love at first sight* notion, but he felt that way when he saw Jennifer in her classroom. Maybe that's why he acted like a jerk then; he didn't know how to deal with his emotions. And he recalled

how he felt when he saw Jennifer the first time, the very first
time. Maybe *love at first sight* was a thing. How else could he
have remembered meeting her fifteen years ago, if that spark
was not there then? But was the coach right? Would she come
around? Two notions were playing tug of war with his mind
and heart. The coach's philosophy of love and family made
sense to him and played to his heart. Yet, his experience had
always told him that he could only count on himself. Which
was right? And did it matter which was right if Jennifer
wouldn't have anything to do with him? With the battle still
raging deep inside of him, he turned his back to Jennifer's
house and escaped to Stephanie's house.

Jennifer was curious as to why it had taken her dad so long
to dispense with Greg. She had heard no shouting. When her
dad came back inside, he seemed as calm as the eye of a
hurricane. His palpable calmness lessened her anxiety, which
was enough to assure her that he had taken care of Greg
sufficiently. "Thanks for going to talk to him, daddy. Wht did
you tell him?

Her dad seemed to put on a layer of resoluteness as he faced her. "Oh, something similar to what I'm going to tell you. Do me a favor and look in your journals. Find one that would have been fifteen years ago in February or March at the end of the wrestling season."

"What?" Jennifer knew that she probably did a double-take at her dad's request. What did any of that have to do with what he said to Greg? And how would he know what was in her journals? Had he read them? She knew that he would not have violated her privacy. More than likely, he knew her well and knew that she wrote almost everything in her journal at that age. Still, she wondered what that had to do with anything going on at the moment. Finally, she voiced her curiosity. "What has that got to do with what you told Greg?"

"Just do me the favor," he replied with an emotionless intonation or expression.

It's Not Fate; It's You

Although Coach Bell said Jennifer would come around, Greg didn't know if that would be the case, and he had to make a decision now. Shortly after noon the next day, Greg stood in Austin's bedroom getting one last look before the taxi came to pick him up to take him to the airport, where a plane would whisk him, and hopefully his memories, away to a nameless, forgettable city. On a wall opposite Austin's bed hung a colorful poster of a self-confident Hunter Savage. Greg imagined Austin waking up every morning seeing this first thing. Greg meandered over to Austin's desk. Two slips of paper showed the name Sparky Gigglepants that Austin frequently insisted he be called. Greg noticed a journal lying beside the slips of paper. It looked like one of the journals the kids used in Ms. Bell's class. Greg picked it up and flipped through it, confirming his hunch that it was used in Ms. Bell's class. As Greg flipped through it, one intriguing heading caught his eye, and he stopped to read that page. The heading was titled, *The Best Day I've Had This Week*. He silently read an excerpt from the journal entry: *My dad showed up at school today for the holiday fun event. I was actually picked to be on a team, and he cheered me on. I actually have friends now. Earlier, I sat on Santa's lap. My dad was dressed up as Santa. He didn't think I recognized him, but I did. I hope he gives me what I wished for.* Greg gently closed the book and wiped his eye with his shirtsleeve.

Greg couldn't bear to stay in the house any longer. The decorations were a painful reminder of what he was giving up; so, he waited outside for the taxi to arrive. Greg heard the front door open, and he looked up to see Stephanie coming out to keep him company. She wore an unbuttoned sweater jacket over top of another sweater. Her arms squeezed her body, and her hands were inside the jacket. She shivered slightly. As soon as she reached Greg, the taxi came into view.

"Are you sure this is what you want to do?" she asked calmly.

"Jennifer doesn't feel the same way for me as I feel for her. I think that's a sign that I need to leave. I've also disappointed Austin ... again. I guess I'm not meant to live the family life." Greg was surprised by the callousness of his own voice.

"Since when have you ever given up on a dream? That's not the Greg Hunter I know."

"I'm not giving up on a dream; I've wanted to be a movie actor for a while."

"Dreams can change. Are you sure this is still the dream you want?"

He wasn't sure anymore, but if the relationship with Jennifer was over and Stephanie was back full-time in Austin's life, he might as well continue down the path of acting. Greg scuffed his shoe along the pavement. When had Stephanie become that wise, or had she always been? "I'm sorry, Stephanie."

"You don't have to apologize to me."

"I do. I wasn't the husband you needed or the father Austin needed me to be. I see now that I was always thinking about myself over my family. The ironic thing is now that I see it, I've lost the opportunity to do anything about it."

"It's not too late. It's not fate that's locking you into this role. It's you."

Even if what Stephanie was saying was true, he just wanted to run away. "Goodbye, Stephanie."

"Goodbye, Greg." Stephanie sighed and tightened the sweater jacket around herself.

Greg recalled Stephanie getting into arguments with him on many occasions, but today she had approached him as a concerned friend who was trying to prevent him from doing something he would later regret.

"Airport, right?" Greg could see the taxi driver's eyes in the rearview mirror.

"Yeah. But first take me to the elementary school. I need to see someone, but I'll only be a few minutes. I'll pay you extra."

"You got it, boss," replied the driver cheerfully.

Within a few minutes, the taxi pulled up to the school drop off area. The little old gatekeeper, as Greg was prone to call her, but not to her face, gave him a jovial wave and indicated that she would sign him in. This late in the afternoon, the kids would be rehearsing for the Christmas Play. Greg arrived in the auditorium in time to see Austin on stage dressed as an angel. To keep from being spotted, Greg sat slumped in a chair with his head low. In this scene, which Greg had seen rehearsed previously, the angel is talking to the protagonist.

Austin's voice was clear and confident as he stated his line. "What does it matter if you have everything," he asked pointing to a stage prop representing riches, "but not the thing that matters the most?"

"What is that?" asked the protagonist in a contemptable tone.

"Family!"

Greg squeezed his eyes shut to trap in the tears. He slinked out of the auditorium and hurried to the taxi … to his escape.

Gone

Stephanie arrived to pick up Austin from the rehearsal, and he was outside waiting for her. Stephanie could tell by the expression on Austin's face that he was upset.

Austin opened the door and climbed into the back seat. Then he tossed his bookbag onto the floorboard and closed the door before buckling his seatbelt. His voice quivered as he asked, "Is dad already gone?"

"He left about an hour ago."

Stephanie anticipated his next question. "He would have waited to leave after you got home, but he had to get to the airport to catch his flight."

"Does dad love me?" Austin's voice broke as he asked the question.

"Austin Hunter," scolded Stephanie. "You know your dad loves you. I know you saw that while he was here."

"But ..."

"No buts. He promised you that he would stay more in touch than he has in the past."

"But what if he doesn't?"

Stephanie sighed. She knew that Austin was probably thinking that making a promise was easier than keeping one. "If he doesn't, then you reach out to him, and if he doesn't respond, reach out to him again. Know that if he is busy, he will respond when he can." Stephanie wondered whether Austin was old enough to understand what she was about to say next; she suspected he was. "A parent should always reach out to their child, no matter the age. But at some point, the child should also accept some responsibility for reaching out to the parent."

"So, it's ok for me to call dad and ask him when he's coming home?"

"Absolutely. You don't have to wait for him to be the first to reach out."

Stephanie could see Austin absorbed in thought as she looked at him through the rearview mirror, and he was quiet the rest of the way home. When they arrived home, Austin slung his bookbag on the floor. Stephanie was about to admonish him to pick it up, but she noticed he was looking at her as if he wanted to talk more.

"I love you, mom. I'm sorry," he said with moist eyes and a catch in his throat.

"I love you too, honey!" Stephanie squatted and mussed his hair with her hand to try to get him to smile. That not working, she asked, "Sorry about what?"

"I wanted dad to fall in love with Ms. Bell."

"He wanted that too. Why are you sorry?"

Austin's lower lip began to quiver, pulling a tear from his eye. "I didn't think about how that would make you feel."

Stephanie fought tears herself. Her eyes were wet, but she forced a smile. "I'm so proud of you. You really are growing up, you know. You considering everyone's feelings is proof of that." Stephanie paused to consider what to say next. "I want your dad to be happy too, and I think he would be very happy with Ms. Bell. I'm not jealous of that."

Austin's lip quivered more, pulling a few more tears down his cheeks. "But I want you to be happy too. You need someone too."

"You don't need to worry about that. When I said as children grew older some of the responsibility was on them, I didn't mean that you needed to worry about me finding someone. Maybe I will, or maybe I won't find someone. I do believe in the old saying that love finds you when you least expect it." Stephanie rose from her squatting position and turned Austin 180 degrees. "I know I shouldn't, but I'm going to let you have one Christmas cookie before dinner." She gave Austin a slight push, and he scurried to the kitchen. "Just one," she reiterated loudly. "I don't want you spoiling your dinner."

Nothing Can be Received unless It is Given

Greg waited in the small reception room of his agent's office and chatted with the pretty receptionist. After arriving in New York City from Cincinnati yesterday, he called up a friend and spent the night at his house. They talked for hours, which was mostly Greg's fault. He knew as soon as he went to bed that he would merely toss and turn all night, which was the case. Greg couldn't stop thinking about Jennifer, wondering what had gone wrong. Was it the fact that he would be on the road most of the time? She had already been there and done that, and she told him that didn't work for her. But something seemed to have happened before he told her he got the movie role. Supposedly, that thing was Helen, but surely Jennifer knew there was nothing between them. He hoped Coach Bell would relay to Jennifer what he had relayed to the coach. Maybe there was something more, something he was overlooking. Perhaps Jennifer had some issues to work out just as he did. Or again, perhaps it was just the fact that he would be gone most of the time. Jennifer was a family person at heart.

Still, she tolerated it with Steve. Now, Greg was feeling childish. Just because she put up with it from one person didn't mean she loved Greg less by no longer wanting to tolerate it again.

Greg's agent threw open the door. "What do you mean by this, Ms. Barnes? We can't keep a famous actor waiting out here like this."

Typical agent thought Greg. The look on Ms. Barnes' face told him that she didn't feel this as chastisement. It probably happened all the time and was just the agent's way of making his client feel more important while he was busy in his office talking with another client.

"Greg, buddy! Come in. Your days of waiting in a lobby are over." His agent tried to put his arm around Greg's shoulders to guide him into the office, but Greg was too tall for the agent to do that, and it came off awkwardly.

No doubt, he is trying to hustle me into his office quickly before his next appointment arrives, thought Greg. Later, he'll shove me out the back door on the pretenses of it being for my sake to avoid reporters. Then, he'll go out and repeat the same spiel with Ms. Barnes. Poor woman. The agent pulled out a chair for Greg at a conference table and held it while he sat. He's pulling out all the stops for me, concluded Greg.

"Let's review the contract the production company sent over. I made sure you got a great deal on this. Depending on the success of the first movie, which is all but guaranteed, you will be under contract to do up to two sequels. The outlook for the first movie is so promising that as soon as it finishes filming, they will begin the sequel. You'll have a small break after the sequel. The executive producer will see how well the first movie is doing at the box office. Then, if all goes well, they'll film the next sequel. During this small break, you can return to professional wrestling for six months or so to continue to build on your popularity. After the final sequel is filmed, we'll of course have you lined up for other movie roles by then."

"Looks like you have my life all planned out," Greg said flatly. The agent obviously hadn't noticed his lack of excitement, thought Greg.

"Yes indeed. We'll have every day committed for the next five years, hopefully longer."

"Sounds like I'm just trading a heavy wrestling commitment for an equally involved acting and wrestling commitment." Greg looked up from the contract to see what he thought was a big fake smile planted on the agent's face. "How long do I have to think about this?" sighed Greg.

The agent's smile disappeared almost instantly, and his eyes shifted from Greg to the contract. "Well, of course you will want your attorney to review this, but I'm telling you it's a great deal. You'll not get a better one. The production company wants this back three days from now. If they don't receive it by then, they could go with their second choice for the lead role. I don't have to tell you how hard I worked for this deal, and this is what you've been wanting for years." The corner of the agent's mouth developed a twitch. "I hear you have a wrestling match tomorrow night."

"Yes. It's in St. Paul and will be aired live on television. I've got a flight out tonight. I have to see the doctor in the morning to get clearance to wrestle. The wrestling promoter told me it would be a short match to give my knee a little more time to recuperate before the next big livestreaming pay-per-view event at *Winter Frenzy*."

"Don't injure your knee. The filming date will not be changed. If you have to be out for surgery, they'll go with another actor, but they're counting on your momentum from *Winter Frenzy* to promote the movie. Give a great show; just don't hurt yourself." As if it were that easy, thought Greg. The agent stood up and glanced at his watch. "Tell you what. Let your lawyer review this while you concentrate on wrestling. Then after the match, make sure you get this contract back to me signed the next morning." Greg stood up, and the agent guided Greg toward a back exit in his office. "Take this door Greg, buddy. It should get you a private getaway. By now, the entertainment reporters probably know you are here and are already lined up at the front entrance."

As Greg slinked out of his agent's office, he noticed several people going into a church, carrying presents and gift-wrapping materials. He remembered the favor Coach Bell asked of him, and he wandered into the church. He followed a group into the church social hall where lots of presents were stored. Volunteers who had arrived earlier had already prepared numerous tables with scissors, boxes, ribbons, and wrapping paper.

"Have you ever wrapped presents before?" asked a kind-looking woman who appeared to be in her sixties."

"Not really," replied Greg. "At least not any that looked decent after I wrapped them."

The woman laughed, showing crow's feet in the corners of her eyes. "Don't worry. I'll show you and give you some tips. Now, I'm not promising you'll be a professional after I show you, but any gifts you wrap will look better than what you described of your previous attempts. By the way, my name is Mira."

"Thank you, Mira. I would appreciate any help you can give me. I'm Greg."

"Pleased to meet you, Greg."

"I'm pleased to meet you too."

Mira spent about fifteen minutes showing Greg how to wrap presents. Then the pastor of the church came in and greeted everyone.

"Get ready," grinned Mira. "Our pastor has to turn everything into a sermon."

Almost as if on cue, the pastor held up his hands to get everyone's attention. "Everyone here knows I'm a man of brevity." Laughter erupted from the crowd, bringing a smile to the pastor's face. "Before we get started, I just wanted to explain why this work is so important. Christmas is a time of miracles. For the kids whose names are on the angel tree, this may be the only present they get this year. These gifts remind them that there are people who care and that they can receive something they've asked for. The same is true though for adults. If you ask from your heart and have faith that you will receive, you can receive a Christmas miracle yourself. Of course, nothing can be received unless it is given. And that's why you are all here tonight … to give so that others can receive. Thank you all for coming out and taking time to help tonight."

When the pastor finished speaking, everyone went to a table and began the task of wrapping presents. Some presents, such as bicycles, only needed a bow. Others required boxes, wrapping paper, and ribbon or bows. Greg was at a table with Mira, and she kept an eye on him, correcting his technique when necessary. After Greg had finished wrapping presents, he helped carry the wrapped presents to a central location.

The time spent wrapping presents went by quickly, and soon all the presents had been wrapped. People began heading out. Greg thanked Mira again for teaching him how to wrap gifts. Although Greg felt uncomfortable going into a church where he knew no one and wrapping presents that he had not really wanted to wrap, he now felt soothed and was glad that he had spent even a short period of time here.

Greg searched for excuses not to go back to his apartment, but he knew he needed to get back since he had an early flight the next day. His apartment had always been his sanctuary. Now, it seemed bitterly lonely and devoid of anything resembling family. It was quite a contrast with Stephanie's house.

Fate or Faith

The next morning in St. Paul, the doctor hired by the GWO gave Greg a clean bill of health with very little examination of his knee. The doctor watched Greg walk, and then he basically just asked Greg a couple of questions about how it felt. Tony was waiting for him outside of the room when he exited.

"Hey, Greg. I'm glad you're back." Tony clapped Greg on the back and shook his hand. "I just wanted to remind you that your match tonight will be quick, between five to ten minutes at most. Take most of that time to strut around and rev up the crowd. Don't perform any moves off the top rope. We don't want to jeopardize your participation at *Winter Frenzy*. As usual, I'll be the play-by-play announcer, and Chris will be the color commentator."

Greg liked Tony. Off camera, he was as genuine a person as you would ever know. "Have you heard the plans yet for *Winter Frenzy?*" queried Greg.

"The organization still plans for you to head the main event. As you know, your contract ends on December 31st, which will give you a clean break to begin your acting career. The plan is for the match to run around thirty minutes, and you'll lose the belt to Rocky Rhodes. They're going to let you keep this belt since you held it for so long. A new one has been made for Rocky. It'll symbolize a new era for the organization. Of course, you can still come back for short periods of time between movies. It will be good for both you and the GWO." Tony grew somber and cast his eyes downward. "I'm going to miss you. We go way back, and it won't be the same here without you. But good luck with acting; I wish you the best."

Greg put his hand on Tony's shoulder. "I feel the same."

That night, Greg stood behind the curtains waiting to go to the wrestling ring. The jobber was already in the ring. Greg had not wrestled a jobber, a wrestler who routinely lost, in a long time. This particular jobber, who was nicknamed Mat, and kidded by some of the wrestlers because his shoulders were always pinned to the mat, had been hand-picked for the match tonight to lessen the chances of Hunter Savage getting injured. He had years of experience and was probably a better wrestler than many of the bigger names. Hunter Savage's entrance music started playing, and Hunter Savage emerged from behind the curtain to a mixture of cheers and boos from the crowd. He twirled around and framed his hands around the GWO championship belt around his waist, which worked the crowd up further. When he set foot into the ring, the bell rang to start the match. To milk some time, Hunter Savage strutted around the ring. As his opponent moved to engage him, Hunter put up both hands to signal a stop. Then in signature fashion, he swept his right hand through his hair on the right side of his head. The cheers and boos grew deafening in the arena. His opponent went for his knee, but Hunter Savage sidestepped him and held up a wagging finger as his opponent turned around. Greg was in his element as Hunter Savage. Hunter had avoided any real wrestling almost entirely, up to the five-minute mark. To milk some more time, he put Mat in a headlock. The referee approached, with a telling look on his face. The referee feigned checking to make sure Hunter wasn't using a choke hold so that he could inform the two wrestlers of some news.

The referee leaned in and whispered, "There's some trouble with the last match, and it's not going to take place. It was scheduled for thirty minutes. Are you ok with going another thirty-five minutes? If not, let me know, and I'll signal to the Live Events Director. I know you need to take care of your knee; so, it's no problem if you want to stop."

"I'm good to go," whispered Greg.

"Me too," whispered Mat.

The referee backed out, appearing to be satisfied that no choke hold was being used.

Suddenly, Jennifer's words popped into his head. *Do you always end the match the same way with the same move? That seems like it would be predictable to an opponent. Why not change it up?* Something seemed to snap in Greg's mind. He couldn't explain what he was thinking, but he suddenly felt very excited. Why not change it up? To most opponents, a change up at this point would be confusing and ill-advised, but this particular opponent was so experienced with so many different wrestlers that Hunter knew he could pull it off.

Greg tied up with his opponent. "Want to put on a show they won't forget anytime soon?" Greg whispered.

His opponent's eyes grew wide, and Greg could see the excitement in them, an excitement that probably hadn't been there in years due to Mat losing continually to bigger names.

Greg strangely wasn't worried about getting hurt. Mat had wrestled so many wrestlers that Greg knew he had learned to go with the flow.

Mat gave a slight nod to indicate his willingness, and Greg mouthed, "Give it all you've got."

For the next thirty minutes, the two exchanged a barrage of high-profile wrestling moves: suplexes, powerbombs, clotheslines, bulldogs, DDTs, submission moves, jawbreakers, and so on.

Tony and Chris did their best to keep up with the action in the ring.

"Mat is fighting like a wildfire against the wind," ventured Tony. "I've never seen this kind of ability from Mat. Hunter Savage is reeling, completely discombobulated and flabbergasted!"

"You're being a little redundant there, aren't you Tony? Are you trying to get all of your vocabulary words for the day into one sentence?" quipped Chris. "I guess Mat is finally tired of being a doormat and is taking it out on the returning champion."

Then the talk would turn to Hunter's momentum.

"This is classic Hunter Savage," squealed Tony. "Like a phoenix rising from the ashes, he's back in the fight. Hunter Savage is the professor, and he's giving Mat a masterclass in butt kicking. He's tearing into Mat like a chainsaw through a Christmas Tree."

"Like Jim Ross used to say, he's beating him like a government mule," bantered Chris. "I tell you, Tony, Mat is tougher than that two-dollar steak your mother cooked all day."

When both Hunter and Mat were equally slugging it out, the two commentators again adjusted their comments with expressions such as: "Each man is turning the ring into their own personal battlefield." Or, "This match is a symphony of destruction with two maestros going toe-to-toe." Or, "This is an all-out demolition derby of destruction in the ring!"

With about five minutes remaining in the match, the referee signaled to the two combatants that it was time to start wrapping up the match.

Tony was calling the play-by-play. "Kick to Hunter's gut by Mat. He's picking Hunter up ... and ... powerbomb. Mat's going outside the ring and is climbing the corner post. If he lands this move, it could be all over for the world champion. Wait, Hunter is getting to his feet. Mat is on the top rope and doesn't see that Hunter is up. Hunter is running to the corner … jumps to the middle rope. Hunter has Mat around the waist. Oh! Overhead belly to belly suplex off the ropes. Beautifully executed. That should be all she wrote for Mat. Hold on! Hunter is not going for the pin."

"Big mistake," called Chris. Hunter knows better than that. Always take the win when you can."

Tony continued with the play-by-play. "The crowd is chanting *Full House*, Hunter's finishing move."

"It doesn't look like he's going for the *Full House*.

"Hunter has Mat in a front facelock."

"What are you doing?" whispered Mat. "This isn't the *Full House*."

"Do you trust me?" whispered Greg.

"I do."

"Just roll with it. I'm not going to hurt you."

Tony continued describing the action in the ring. "Hunter is grabbing Mat's tights and hoisting him up. It looks like he's going to do a vertical suplex." With what transpired next, Tony was speechless to call the action. Hunter performed a different move that even caught the referee off guard. Matt executed it equally as well. The crowd grew eerily silent for a split second before erupting into the loudest cheering Greg had ever heard; he couldn't hear a single boo. The noise jolted the dumbfounded referee, and he sprang to the mat to make the three count.

"I've never seen anything like that," blurted Chris. "What do you even call that?"

"I've never seen that move before. Hunter had him up for a vertical suplex and then dropped Mat, using the top rope as a slingshot into what I'll just call a hanging neckbreaker and then into a sitout neckbreaker."

Hunter's opponent whispered to him, "It was a privilege to be in the ring with you, and I would wrestle against you anytime."

"Same here," replied Hunter.

After the last of the remaining crowd had dwindled from the arena, Tony came into the dressing room as Greg had showered and dressed in street clothes. "Man, that was some finisher. I've never seen it, and we didn't even know what to call it! We were as excited as the crowd, and I haven't seen that kind of reaction from a crowd in a long time."

"Seeing how this is one of my last matches, I wanted to end with a bang."

"It was certainly that, and Mat followed it perfectly."

"You know. Mat is really a great wrestler. It's a shame he's never been in the limelight. Maybe you could try to push him with the higher ups."

"That might be a hard sell, given his long history of losing."

Greg folded his arms and looked directly at Tony.

"I'll see what I can do," Tony replied sheepishly. "I'm not one of the higher ups."

Greg remained in his pose, continuing to stare at Tony.

"Ok. Ok." Tony yielded to Greg's imposing look. "I'll push him as a favor to you."

"You're the best, Tony."

"Several of the wrestlers are going to a bar in a few minutes. Are you going?"

"I rented a Porshe today. I want to drive it before I have to turn it in in the morning. You know, I don't get a chance to drive much, especially sports cars."

"You and those cars. The playboy life really suits you. What's it like living in the limelight?"

Greg grew quiet and serious looking, and Tony began to shift. Greg spoke quietly, almost dreamily. "Ah, there's one thing about the limelight, Tony. It exposes you and takes away all the shadows you used to hide in."

Tony tilted his head to the side and wore a puzzled expression. Greg didn't want to even try to explain to Tony what he meant by his comment; so, he just threw up a wave and patted Tony on the back.

"See you at *Winter Frenzy*," called Tony. "You know with that new move, I wouldn't be surprised if they let you win at *Winter Frenzy* and go out undefeated as the world champion."

The night was hazy and had obscured the skylight. The only visible light was from the city and the traffic. The air was cold, definitely December-like. A million thoughts seemed jumbled in Greg's mind, and he wanted nothing more than to escape the city and drive until his mind quieted. As he awkwardly maneuvered his large frame into the small Porshe's driver seat, his mobile phone, which he carried in his front pocket, jabbed his lower abdomen. He took it out and saw a message from his agent. *Greg, buddy, great match tonight. I need that signed contract first thing in the morning. Get ready for the ride of your life.* Closing the message app, he noticed that the photo app had somehow been opened. The photo displayed on his phone was of Jennifer wearing his world championship wrestling belt. Thumbing quickly though some photos, he saw one of Jennifer in her silver dress. Greg closed the app and tossed the phone onto the passenger seat. Soon he was on the highway headed out of the city. He knew he was driving faster than he should, but there was little traffic this time of night. He hoped no highway patrol was around.

Greg was poised to get everything he had wanted for the past ten or more years. Why was he now questioning it? He knew why. He had never slowed down enough to think. His brief time with Austin and Jennifer had allowed him to slow down, to think, to question the man he had become and the life he was living. Was he sabotaging his own future? Thoughts of Jennifer and Austin kept invading his brain. He hadn't spoken to either one. He told himself, the reason was to keep from clouding his judgement. But his judgement was clouded, nonetheless. He used to tell Stephanie that when he made it big in professional wrestling, he would have more time for family. Now he could just substitute acting in place of wrestling, and he was telling the same story, the same lie. There would be no more time for Austin. In fact, there would be less time if the movie sequels were made. He wanted both family and fame, but the two were polar opposites; there was no way of bringing them together.

Remembering what the pastor said at the church where he wrapped presents yesterday, Greg spoke his dilemma aloud, a prayer to God for guidance, for a Christmas miracle in his life. "What am I doing? What should I do?" Greg was now driving on a lonely highway enveloped in darkness. His attention turned to the radio, and he turned it on as if God would answer him through that medium. Greg let out a sinister laugh when he heard the song that was playing, *Runaway Train* by Soul Asylum. God must have a sense of humor, he thought. The song described him perfectly. Just like the song described, he was in too deep and had led himself astray making promises that he couldn't keep. Was he a runaway train that was never going back? Was he headed the wrong way on a one-way track, neither here nor there? So that was God's answer, telling him what he already knew and felt. His prayer was to no avail. He slammed his fist on the steering wheel. His fuming gradually turned to depression. He knew that feeling sorry for himself was not helping to bring about a solution, but somehow it felt good. He supposed that was the reason behind blues and sad songs.

The last stage in the five stages of grief was acceptance. Was that what he was going to have to do?" Just accept his fate? The word *fate* triggered another word in his mind from the pastor. That word was *faith*. Then, he remembered that he had asked two questions. The first one was, *What was he doing?* The Runaway Train song told him perfectly what he was doing. Had he stopped too soon? Would God speak to him through the radio a second time, granting the Christmas miracle he hoped for? Excitement, like electricity, tingled through his body. He fidgeted in the car seat, experiencing both expectancy and trepidation. He randomly pressed a preset on the radio and was caught in the silence between the station changes. When the song finally came on, tears streamed from his eyes. He was crying like a baby; he hadn't cried since he was a teenager. The tears blurred his eyes so badly that he had to pull the Porshe to the side of the road. Playing on the radio was the song, *I'll be home for Christmas*.

If the Bud is There, It Can Still Bloom

Jennifer stood at the door to Stephanie's house, trying to decide whether to ring the doorbell or go back home. She hadn't seen Stephanie since Stephanie got back from training in London. She knew the neighborly thing to do, especially near Christmas, was to see Stephanie. But she was conflicted, to say the least. She had tried to keep her promise to Stephanie, and she had done so to a great extent. She made sure Greg did Christmas activities with Austin, and she kept an eye on Greg. She was pretty sure though that Stephanie had not meant for her to keep an eye on him to such an extent as to fall in love with her ex-husband. Jennifer was almost too embarrassed to set eyes on Stephanie.

Jennifer was really at Stephanie's door for another mission though. In her hands, she held Austin's coat that had been left at her house. She knew Austin had other coats; she had seen him wear them. That was no reason though to keep this one from him just so that she could save herself from some embarrassment.

She finally collected enough courage to ring the doorbell, either that or her hands were becoming numb from her indecisiveness. Stephanie opened the door just in time to receive a cloud of breath in her face coming from Jennifer's cold body.

"Jennifer, you look as though you are about frozen. Hurry and get inside."

Jennifer hurried into the warm house and felt as though she were instantly beginning to thaw out. The Christmas fragrance from baking and from fresh pine greeted Jennifer's nose, warming her even further.

"Austin left this at my house." Jennifer held up the coat as though she needed to explain the reason for her visit. She tried to be funny by adding, "I wanted to return it before Kringle decided it was his," but it fell flat when she said it.

A flash of light from around Stephanie's neck caught Jennifer's eyes, and she noticed a necklace identical to the one she saw Greg buy and identical to the one she had seen Helen wear. "Where did you get that?" she asked, trying not to sound impertinent.

Stephanie flashed a smile that melted away any remaining defenses Jennifer had put up. "It's beautiful, isn't it? I really shouldn't be wearing it now sine it's supposed to be a Christmas present. Greg bought it when he was with you and Austin as a Christmas present from Austin to me."

Stephanie didn't seem upset about Greg's and Jennifer's feelings toward each other. And now she knew for certain that Greg was telling the truth about the necklace. She wondered why Helen had not simply told her the truth when she asked her directly about it.

"Thank you for helping Austin," continued Stephanie. "He seems to be doing better socially now."

"He has, and you don't have to thank me. It was his ... uh... his dad really who helped him." Jennifer saw Stephanie look at her hands. Jennifer was playing with her hands much the same way that Greg did when he was nervous.

"Last night, ... uh ... Greg wrestled on tv. I just wondered if anyone kidded Austin again about it."

"Oh. I didn't know ... I mean no. No one teased him that I'm aware of."

"I also want to thank you for Greg."

Jennifer's eyes widened at Stephanie's comment.

"Look, I know it's none of my business what happened between you two," admitted Stephanie, "but Greg was a different person, and you had a lot to do with that. He's always been a good man, just misguided. You've been the only person to bring out the kind of man he could be, and I appreciate that for Austin's sake."

Jennifer felt nervous and wanted to flee the house, but she stood her ground. Stephanie had been a good friend, and she didn't want to lose that friendship. Jennifer mustered the courage to ask what had been on her mind. "Did he say anything about me?"

Jennifer had blurted out the question so quickly, that to Stephanie, it seemed almost like it was one long word. She turned around. Jennifer's clutched hands below her waist, the quick in and out of her chest from shallow breathing, the eager anticipation in her eyes, and the paleness of her face told Stephanie that it had taken a lot for Jennifer to ask this of her.

Stephanie could feel the tenseness in her own shoulders give way, allowing a smile to appear on her face. She walked closer to Jennifer, close enough to take Jennifer's hands in her own. "Let's have a seat, shall we?"

Jennifer's head bobbed up and down a couple of times in agreement. The two women sat next to each other on the couch. Stephanie wasn't sure what to say, but she said a quick and silent prayer that what she did say would work to everyone's benefit. With renewed confidence, Stephanie now felt that perhaps Jennifer would confide in her. "He said that he loved you." Jennifer gasped quickly. "He meant it," added Stephanie, "and I believe him. As I said, I know it's none of my business what happened between the two of you, but for the first time in Greg's life, he was in love." Jennifer stuttered trying to say something. "You're thinking it's really weird for an ex-wife to be talking to another woman about her ex-husband like this, aren't you."

Jennifer let out a deep sigh that immediately loosened her shoulders and allowed the words to come out naturally. "I am."

"Don't worry. I'm not jealous that he never felt that way about me. We were friends who should have stayed friends. Well, I take that back. I know it's cliché, but I'm thankful he gave me Austin. I'm so glad for Austin that I wouldn't trade anything for him. What I'm trying to say is that I see two good people who are hurting. I know he loves you, and I suspect you feel the same about him. If there's some way to bring the two of you together, I want to help. Really."

Stephanie could see the reluctance fade from Jennifer's body. Her shoulders straightened, and she looked like the fourth-grade teacher Stephanie knew her to be.

"There are two things standing in the way of that happening. I had an ex-boyfriend, Steve, who was a workaholic like Greg. We were rarely together and rarely spent any quality time with each other. I had just grown accustomed to that until I realized that I wanted more. Steve was unable to give me the commitment I wanted. I see the same thing with Greg."

Stephanie sighed, wondering how to address this. Stephanie wondered if Greg could make that commitment. She certainly thought he could and would with Jennifer, but she knew that only Greg could determine that, and he wasn't there to say. "I wish I could say something to alleviate your concerns, but I'm afraid I can't. I can only say that Greg was a different person for a while because of you. If he could make a commitment with anyone, it would be with you. Whether he allows himself to do that, I just don't know." Stephanie stopped talking, hoping to read Jennifer's mannerisms. Then she remembered that Jennifer said two things. "You said there was another thing standing in the way." She phrased it as a statement rather than a question, but she hoped that Jennifer would take that as an invitation to tell her.

Jennifer hesitated momentarily. "I don't know how to ask this. Is Greg the playboy that he appears to be on tv? He's popular, extroverted, and good-looking. He has women around him and certainly opportunity."

Stephanie snorted and put her hand over her mouth and nose to hide the uncontrollable laughter. "Oh my," she managed to say through the laughter. She cleared her throat to prevent another snort and to give herself time to stop laughing. "Those women are just part of the show. If one of them behaved that way in real life toward Greg, he would run away so fast that his shadow couldn't even catch him. He may seem like a playboy, but that is certainly not who he is. I know you're thinking I don't see him enough to know, but know him I do."

Jennifer's eyebrows creased and her nose scrunched up. Stephanie knew she had something on her mind.

"It just doesn't make sense," replied Jennifer, as if she had read Stephanie's thoughts. "He wanted to meet me for coffee. When I arrived, I saw him with Helen Collins. They had apparently been shopping together. They were hugging each other, and she wore a necklace that I saw him buy at a Christmas Market. My dad told me that Greg said she just happened to show up, and I understand about the necklace now. I'm just not sure I'm convinced about Helen."

"That was the day he went to see you," replied Stephanie, thinking back. "He had just told me that he loved you. I wish I could explain what you saw, but I do know that he loves only you. He certainly doesn't care for Helen. It was you he couldn't stop talking about. She couldn't explain Greg hugging Helen, but she imagined it was an innocent gesture that Jennifer spied at the wrong moment. Greg could seem uncaring, but underneath he hid a big sympathetic heart that seemed to get him in trouble, which was probably why he tried not to show that he cared. "Have you spoken to Helen since that day?"

"No. Both of us have been trying to avoid each other as much as possible. At least, I know I have, and there have been times that Helen has turned around or pretended to be busy to avoid me."

Stephanie reached out and covered Jennifer's hand with her own. "Talk to Helen, but especially talk to Greg. Please."

Jennifer fixed her gaze on the floor as she spoke and leaned back into the couch, withdrawing her hands. "I don't know. I think the moment has passed. I think the damage is irreparable."

"If there is real love there, don't you think you owe it to both you and Greg to give it a chance to blossom? If the bud is there, it can still bloom."

Jennifer stood from the couch. "There is still the issue of commitment. I need to see that from Greg. I can't stand for my heart to break further."

Stephanie stood up as Jennifer started to leave. Then, she remembered one more thing she wanted to say. "You were partially correct; Greg did buy a gift for another woman." Pulling out the gift-wrapped box containing the silver bell pendant, necklace, and earrings, she handed it to Jennifer. The adhesive gift label showed *To Jen, From Greg* and was written in Greg's handwriting. "Greg bought this for you." Jennifer's mouth stood open, and her eyes were moist. "I told him that he needed to give this to you himself, but he left it at the house. I thought you should have it." Stephanie knew that she had given it her best shot. There was nothing left to say. Kismet, or a Christmas miracle, would have to do its work now if the two were to come together. Stephanie forced a smile on her face. "Merry Christmas, Jennifer."

Night of the Play

On the night of Austin's Christmas Play, Stephanie tried to pin Austin down so that she could put the cloak costume on him. She finally managed to overcome his squirming; at least he was partially dressed for the play. She didn't dare attach the wings; they would be smushed before they made it to the auditorium.

"Are you going to record the play for dad?" Austin had asked this same question several times over the past few days.

Stephanie replied with the same answer that she had every other time when Austin asked this question. "It's being recorded by the school, but I'll video the parts you're in so that he'll have a close up."

"M ... Mom? D ... Do you think d ... dad gets nervous before matches?"

Stephanie could have kicked herself. She should have known that Austin would make the comparison with his dad, and she should have prepared something thoughtful ahead of time to tell him. Now, she would have to wing it. "I'm sure he does, sometimes. Children aren't always like their parents though. Sometimes they are opposites, and just because your dad is a great performer in front of people doesn't mean you are supposed to be just like him. You are good at things he's not good at. Besides, he's had years of practice." To give a little extra reassurance, she added, "I'm sure you'll do great. I have confidence in you."

Austin peered into his mom's face. Dressed in a white cloak, Stephanie thought this was the closest thing she had ever seen to a real angel. She framed his face with her hands and kissed his forehead.

"Mom! You're going to mess me up before we get to the school."

That was the sign that he would be okay. Stephanie chuckled to herself that all of his squirming wasn't going to mess up his costume, but her giving a motherly kiss would. Boys. "I want you to eat a small amount of food before we leave."

Austing scrunched up his eyes and nose. "Why?"

"If you don't eat anything, your stomach will be growling before the end of the performance, and people want be able to hear you over your stomach." Stephanie poked his stomach. Austin giggled and jumped back, covering his stomach, almost involuntarily. "If you eat too much and then get nervous, it could make you sick, and then ... well ... you know."

Austin nodded his head. Apparently, his mom's explanations made complete sense.

Around seven o'clock that evening, they arrived at the school and found many parents and children had already arrived. Austin pulled at the door handle before Stephanie put the car in park. He yanked it again several times.

"Calm down, honey. We've arrived in plenty of time."

When Stephanie finally unlocked the doors, Austin yanked again at the handle and sprinted out of the car. Stephanie noticed that he had forgotten to take the rest of his costume.

"Honey! You forgot part of your costume."

Several kids alternated looking between Austin and Stephanie, and Stephanie discerned Austin's red-cheeked embarrassment as he turned around. Ah, the embarrassment a mother could bring to her child. It was as timeless as Christmas.

He shuffled back to the car with his head down. "Mom." He spoke through a barely open mouth as a ventriloquist would. "You don't have to embarrass me."

Stephanie handed him the angel wings with attached halo. "I think you would be more embarrassed to be on stage with only part of your costume." Stephanie's logic hadn't seemed to work on Austin. He grabbed the wings, clutching them to his chest, and he glanced around several times. Stephanie assumed he was looking to see if anyone was still looking at him. Stephanie bent down to kiss his cheek.

"Mom!"

There was the ventriloquist voice again; so, she stopped short of kissing him. "Good luck," she whispered.

"Mom!"

"Oh." Stephanie quickly covered her mouth with her hand and just as quickly removed it. "Break a leg." Austin scampered into the school auditorium.

It was still a little early to go in. Stephanie wanted a good seat, but she still had plenty of time. Although a good number of parents had already arrived, they were milling around talking with one another. It was a little cool, but not as cold as it had been the past couple of nights. The interlude between getting Austin to the school and the beginning of the play allowed Stephanie time to think. Unfortunately, her thoughts turned to Greg. Although he hadn't been gone too long, he had yet to call Austin. So much for his renewed promise. Perhaps Jennifer's magic had worn off, but she didn't really believe that. More than likely, he was still hurting and licking his wounds. That was still no excuse for not contacting Austin. Stephanie realized she was clenching her fists, and just like Austin had done, she glanced around to see if anyone was watching. Perhaps she should go in and find a seat before her thoughts led her in a wrong direction, especially during the Christmas season.

The school auditorium was decorated nicely for Christmas. It was quite homey for a school. Stephanie chose a seat a few rows back from the front. She wanted to be close, but the first row was almost too close up to see the entire stage. After waiting for about thirty minutes, the lights in the auditorium flickered several times. The play was almost ready to start. Parents, siblings of the kids in the play, and friends began to filter into the rows of seating as they finished up their conversations or made one last trip to the restroom.

From behind the curtain Ms. Bell emerged. Even Stephanie had to admit she looked stunning. The red dress she wore was very Christmassy.

Ms. Bell began her remarks. She laid out the rules of manner that the audience was to observe, and to silence their phones. She reminded everyone that the play was being recorded and that a link to the recording would be provided in about one week's time. "I want to thank everyone for coming out tonight. The kids have really put in a lot of work into this play. I would also like to thank the set designers and volunteers for helping everything come together. I hope you enjoy the show." Smiling broadly, she exited through the curtains. The audience grew quiet, and the curtains spread. The show was about to begin.

What's Your Tagline Now?

Greg quietly opened the doors and then gently closed
them. Darn, the play had begun already. He glanced at his
watch. 8:03 PM. Hopefully, he had only missed three minutes
at most. Scanning the first few rows, he spotted Stephanie.
That's Steph. She always wanted to be up close but not the first
or second row. And there was a vacant seat beside of her. He
walked at a brisk pace to the row where Stephanie sat and
worked his large frame past several people, apologizing along
the way and trying to avoid stepping on people's toes.
Stephanie did not look over until he sat in the empty seat
beside her. She probably would not have looked then had he
not bumped her arm when he sat. Why did public seating
always have to have seats so close to each other and be just a
tad too small? When Stephanie did look over, she did a double
take, and her jaw dropped. Greg was tempted to take his hand
and close her mouth, but the adult in him won out over the
adolescent, and he refrained from doing so.

"What happened? What are you doing here?" she
whispered.

"I couldn't do it. I couldn't leave our son."

"Shh!" came a voice from behind them. Greg's whisper wasn't as hushed as Stephanie's.

Greg couldn't tell if the smile on Stephanie's face was because he had just been admonished or because he was actually there. Probably a little bit of both.

"Or his teacher?" she added.

Now it was Greg's turn to smile. Stephanie knew him well.

"I'm happy for you," exclaimed Stephanie.

"Shh!" insisted the voice behind them.

The look on Stephanie's face told Greg that she genuinely was happy for him. He searched for Jennifer, but he knew she was backstage, or stage right, or stage left, or wherever except in plain view. Turning his attention to the play, he began to get into the story he had read in Jennifer's manuscript.

The play centered around two individuals. One was a self-employed handyman, who didn't charge a lot to help those in need. He did lot of small, good deeds such as helping a scout leader with a barbeque sale, helping a girl put up a basketball goal, and taking a day off work to watch the sick child of a friend who couldn't take off from work. The main protagonist was the CEO of a large business, who was only out to make a profit and who rarely helped the community. A Christmas angel showed the CEO what it would have been like if he had never been born and what it was like to see life through the eyes of the handyman. In one scene, the protagonist looked down and out as the handyman. He was poorly dressed and barely making ends meet. As he walked on a sidewalk, he was approached by the scout leader, the girl, and the friend. He was shown the chain of events from these small acts of kindness that led to better things for others. As the protagonist exited stage, he was heard saying, "the smallest acts of kindness really do make a difference."

After the play was over, Austin saw his parents and ran to them. Austin put an arm around each parent. "Dad! I can't believe you came. You're both here! How did I do?"

"You were wonderful, sweetie." Stephanie bent over and hugged her son, kissing him on the top of his head.

"Mom, don't embarrass me in front of everyone."

Greg stood straight with his hands on his hips, beaming with pride. "Your mom's right. I need to take acting lessons from you!"

Wide eyes pleading, Austin looked up at his dad. "Are you staying?"

"Forever."

Austin grabbed as high up to his father as he could and clung tightly. Greg picked him up in the air, hugging him tightly, and Stephanie wrapped her arms around them both. They were all in one big group hug.

"Mom, dad. You're both embarrassing me now." All three laughed, and Greg set him down.

"If you will both excuse me." He didn't have time to finish his sentence.

"Go get her, dad!" interrupted Austin.

Stephanie put a hand on Greg's arm, halting him. "Are you really ready to commit to her? That's what it's going to take to get her back."

"I know," replied Greg, seriously, "and I am."

"Break a leg."

Greg knew that was a show biz saying, but it caused him to think about the knee he had injured. If Jennifer will have me, it's well worth the trade off, he thought to himself jokingly.

Jennifer did not come out to take a bow at the end of the play. As Greg headed backstage, he saw a flower vendor and bought a dozen red roses. Backstage, he quickly found Jennifer. Her back was turned to him, and she was alone, fiddling with some prop. He moved furtively behind her, taking small steps on tiptoes. He cleared his throat, and Jennifer spun around, wide-eyed with a vein in the side of her neck palpitating. He could see that he had startled her.

"Like I said before, a great teacher and a great writer."

"What are you doing here?"

Greg couldn't tell if she was being sarcastic, if her tone was from her being startled, or if she was angry. He tried handing her the roses, but she didn't take them. Perhaps he did have his work cut out for him, but he wasn't going to give up.

"I thought you were training for your match and getting ready for the movie."

"There is a better deal for me here." Greg hoped his confidence would seal the deal with Jennifer. "And it's not with Helen. It's with you, if you'll have me." Greg repeated the story to Jennifer that he had told her father. "I hope your dad told you what I told him. Helen happened to come by the coffee shop while I was outside waiting for you. She dropped two of her shopping bags, and I picked them up. I saw her necklace and commented it was exactly like the one I bought Austin to give to his mom. She asked about coffee, and I said I couldn't. I cared for someone else. She knew it was you. She said you were a wonderful woman, and she hugged me as a friend. That's all. Aside from the one date with Helen that I told you was only to make you jealous, you know I've never shown any interest in Helen." There were a lot of strange coincidences, but it was the truth, and Greg hoped she would believe him.

"I know. I saw Stephanie with the necklace you bought, and Helen said you told her you loved me. I also found out, from dad, that I wrote about meeting you in my journal fifteen years ago."

"He gave me a tip that made me remember meeting you then."

"If only we would have known then, huh?"

"I've never felt with anyone the way I feel about you. My career meant everything to me because I didn't see what I was really missing until Austin, and you showed me. I'm retiring from wrestling after my last match at *Winter Frenzy*. I've already told the CEO, and I turned down the role in the movie. Acting would have continued to take up most of my time, and I would have seen Austin even less. I have a job as a social studies and language arts teacher here at the school. An opening came available because the teacher is transferring to another school to replace a teacher who is retiring after Christmas. And I will be the new wrestling coach for the high school team."

Greg could see the amazed, almost bewildered, look on Jennifer's face.

"Why did you give it all up?"

"Because the woman I love expects who she's with to commit to her, and I want to commit more than anything. You're worth the risk. I had to bet everything I had."

"You love me?" The phrase that Greg said finally seemed to dawn on Jennifer. *You love me?*

Greg couldn't describe the look on Jennifer's face. It was a mixture of shock, excitement, and joy. "Yes. I thought it was obvious. I love you Jennifer Bell, and I can't imagine my life without you. The dream I thought I wanted paled in comparison to what I experienced in real life. To me, I didn't give up anything. As you wrote in the play, what's the point of having it all, if you don't have what really counts?"

Jennifer threw her arms around Greg's neck. "I love you too. Every time I tried to tell you something always seemed to come up, or my own insecurities got in the way. By the way, I've got some exciting news for you too."

Greg couldn't help but kid Jennifer. "You also quit your job to go to the GWO as a female wrestler to be near me? And you liked the look of the world championship belt around you."

"No, silly." Jennifer grabbed his ear, twisting and pulling.

"Ouch. That's a pretty good start on a submission hold."

She pulled a little harder.

"Ok. Ok. I give. What's your news?"

"I contacted the agent who got a publishing deal for me years ago. She contacted the same publisher, and they are willing to publish my book. Plus, I signed a contract for three more books."

"Congratulations! We both have what we want."

"You've finally stopped wrestling with Christmas."

The truth in that statement resonated with Greg. He had stopped wrestling with Christmas, and he had lost, or rather, he had won. By giving in to the Christmas spirit, he had gained a new perspective on family and love for others, one he promised himself that he wouldn't lose. Greg's heartbeat quickened as he wrapped his arms around Jennifer. Enveloped in his embrace, Greg felt Jennifer's arms pin him tightly against her.

"I love you, Jennifer Bell!"

"And I love you, Greg Hunter!"

Greg loved hearing his voice say those words to Jennifer. He had longed to say those words, and within a few minutes he had said them several times, the feeling growing with each repetition. And hearing those words from Jennifer made him feel that his new dream was now possible. "You know. If we married, your last name could be Bell Hunter." For a split second, Greg worried that perhaps he had moved too quickly mentioning marriage, even though he was convinced that their relationship would move in that direction, but Jennifer didn't bat an eyelash. Instead, her smile grew.

"Still finding ways to make fun of my last name, but that sounds better than *Savage*," she remarked.

"I've traded those days for much better ones. I've finally met my match." He truly had, and it was the greatest match he had ever had.

"Well, Mr. The Best Player in the Game. What's your tagline going to be now?"

Greg thought for a second. His usual ability to come back quickly with a quip didn't seem to be working at this moment, and concentrating was difficult as he stared into Jennifer's large, hazel eyes. Finally, one came to him. "I'm no longer a player in the game. Your love has made me tame."

Jennifer's mouth quivered between a smile and an outright laugh. Her twinkling eyes conveyed the amusement that Greg was feeling himself. "That's pretty bad!" she finally managed to say.

"It is pretty bad, isn't it?"

Jennifer's allure numbed his mind completely, leaving a single thought. Greg leaned in, and Jennifer mirrored his movement. Greg's Christmas miracle had come true as they kissed.

Epilogue After All, I am Ms. Christmas!

One Year Later

Greg finished wrestling practice for the day with the high school team. The first few days, he had been a little rusty, but the team was so excited about being coached by a former professional wrestler that they didn't seem to notice. Greg was amazed at how much he enjoyed teaching and coaching. Fame paled in comparison to his newfound sense of belonging. This particular day, he had brought in a guest, Mat from the GWO, who was now the reigning United States Champion. Tony had been good on his promise to push Mat to management. Because Mat had lost so many matches, the storyline was that Hunter Savage personally trained him, and Mat's signature finishing move was the move that Hunter Savage had used on Mat at Hunter's last match. Mat had been an excellent amateur wrestler, and he gave some good tips to the high school wrestling team. As Mat was leaving to catch a plane to head to the next wrestling event, he thanked Greg profusely for helping him with his career, and he told Greg he would be happy to come back anytime Greg wanted.

The wrestling team headed for the locker room, and Greg looked up to see Jennifer, who had snuck in unnoticed. "What a surprise! I thought you would be rehearsing for the school Christmas play, either that or planning our wedding." He kissed Jennifer and stood back to admire her. His love for her continued to grow each day.

"Well, now that Helen is co-directing, I was able to leave early."

"I'm glad that you and Helen have patched things up so well. So, why did you take off early?"

"I, or I should say we, promised Stephanie that we would do something with Austin tonight while she goes on her date. This makes several dates now. Stephanie and her boyfriend seem to be getting along very well." Jennifer shifted in place, swaying from one leg to the other.

"I know that look. You have some other news to tell, don't you?"

"I do! My book is doing well, and they are going to adapt it to a movie, which will begin filming this summer."

"That's wonderful news!"

Jennifer continued to shift in place.

"There's more?" asked Greg.

"I was able to offer a suggestion for the protagonist, and I suggested you. Filming will only take about six weeks. Since it's during the summer when you're out of school, I thought you might want to do it. But you have to promise that you won't let the limelight take you away from me."

"I would never let that happen. There's no going back to that lifestyle for me. I'm too happy."

"Would you at least give it some thought. We could both go on location in Vancouver, B.C."

"If that would make you happy, I would be glad to do it." Greg decided to change the subject to something he was more interested in. "Now, tell me about our wedding."

"I've picked out the dress, and everything is on track. You and I have already picked out everything we want. One added bonus is that my mom is now pressing Carol about getting married."

"I still find it hard to believe that we're getting married on Christmas Day!"

Jennifer batted her eyes. "After all, I am Ms. Christmas!"

About the Author

Dewey Dellinger is an educator and administrator. He was born, raised, and lives in North Carolina and has degrees from North Carolina State University, the University of North Carolina at Charlotte, and East Carolina University. His highest degree is a Ph.D. from North Carolina State University. His novel genres include fantasy, action-adventure, romance and romantic comedy, and drama.

Books by Dewey

Once Upon a Knight's Time Series

Once Upon a Knight's Time

Once Upon a Knight's Time: Seeker of the Sword

Romance

Love's Trail in Kenya

Christmas Romantic Comedy

Wrestling with Christmas

Christmas Drama

Gifts to the Prodigal

Action Heroine

Captain Tomorrow